PUFFIN BOOKS

A CHRISTMASAURUS CAROL

A CHRISTMASAURUS CAROL

TOM FLETCHER

Illustrations by Shane Devries

PUFFIN

PUFFIN BOOKS

UK | USA | Canada | Ireland | Australia
India | New Zealand | South Africa

Puffin Books is part of the Penguin Random House group of companies
whose addresses can be found at global.penguinrandomhouse.com.

www.penguin.co.uk   www.puffin.co.uk   www.ladybird.co.uk

First published 2023
001

Cover, illustrations and text copyright © Tom Fletcher, 2023
Illustrations by Shane Devries

The moral right of the author has been asserted

Text design by Dynamo Limited
Printed in Great Britain by Clays Ltd, Elcograf S.p.A.

The authorized representative in the EEA is Penguin Random House Ireland,
Morrison Chambers, 32 Nassau Street, Dublin D02 YH68

A CIP catalogue record for this book is available from the British Library

HARDBACK
ISBN: 978–0–241–59587–9

INTERNATIONAL PAPERBACK
ISBN: 978–0–241–59588–6

All correspondence to:
Puffin Books, Penguin Random House Children's
One Embassy Gardens, 8 Viaduct Gardens, London SW11 7BW

'*For it is good to be children sometimes, and
never better than at Christmas . . .*'
Charles Dickens, *A Christmas Carol*

You are about to go on a
CHRISTMAS ADVENTURE
with:

William Trundle
The boy who has saved Christmas three times but is still called Willypoos by his dad!

Brenda Payne
William's sister, who is still nice rather than naughty.

Pamela Payne
Brenda's mum, who tries to love Christmas as much as the rest of the family.

Bob Trundle
William's dad and owner of far too many Christmas trees!

Lucy and Larry Dungston,
who might look a bit familiar . . .

Eddie Shepherd
A Holly Jolly Jingler with the voice of an angel (much to William's dismay!).

Santa
Because what's a Christmas adventure without the big man himself?

The Christmasaurus
A very special blue dinosaur with the magic of Christmas in his heart.

Oh, and not forgetting the villain of our story . . .
Ebenezer Scrooge!
The most un-Christmassy person you could ever, ever imagine.

CONTENTS

IT ALL BEGAN
AT CHRISTMAS

I suppose you are expecting this book to be a fun, festive adventure, with a flying blue dinosaur, Santa, elves, William Trundle and all the other things you would usually find in a Christmasaurus story.

Well, I've got good news and bad news.

The good news is that all that *is* going to happen! Dinosaurs, Santa, the whole jingle.

The *bad* news is that in order to tell you *that* story, I must first tell you a little bit of another one.

Now, I know what you're thinking – *starting a story with a totally different story seems a bit silly*, and you're right. It *is* a bit daft. But it's very important. In fact, Christmas itself depends on it.

Why?

Because stories are powerful.

Some stories are *so* powerful that they leap out of their own books and into the pages of others.

Some characters are so good – or, in this case, so *bad* – that they find themselves floating out of their books altogether and into the minds and hearts and imaginations of the reader (that's you!), and crossing into the real world.

But I'm getting ahead of myself. Let's get back to this story . . . I mean, the *other* story.

It all began at Christmas

in London a long, long time ago. A time when there were horses and carts instead of cars and buses, coal fires instead of nice toasty radiators, and chocolate selection boxes hadn't been invented yet, so children had to make do with roasted chestnuts.

This cold, frosty old city was warmed by the familiar signs of Christmas that we still have today. Holly wreaths hung on doors, children made snowmen in the park while their parents stole kisses under sprigs of mistletoe (gross!) and the smell of mince pies wafted from the busy shops.

'Merry Christmas!' said one gentleman to another with a tip of his tall top hat, which people used to wear instead of woolly bobble hats in those days, and in the distance a Christmas carol was being sung by a choir of children as they went from door to door, spreading seasonal cheer.

It was as Christmassy as a picture on a Christmas card!

But don't get too excited, as someone was about to enter this festive scene who was as *un*-Christmassy as you could possibly imagine.

Click-clack.

Click-clack.

His hard footsteps on the cold cobbles caught the attention of a small child in the park.

'It's *him*!' the boy whispered.

'He's coming!' Another child trembled, quickly stuffing a carrot into her snowman's face before dashing to find her parents.

Click-clack.

Click-clack.

As the footsteps got closer, the flames from the street lamps cast the grim shadow of this miserable man on to the walls, which seemed to glaze over with a fresh layer of frost as he approached.

The jolly jumble of Christmas shoppers scrambled inside the buildings to avoid him, and whispers of his name seemed to conjure an icy wind that howled along the streets, blowing wreaths off the doors, snuffing out candles and carrying the merry sounds of Christmas away into the night.

It was as though his very presence was enough to extinguish any sign of Christmas. Even the snowman's nose fell off as this ghastly gentleman passed.

He was tall; at least, he would have been if he had stood up straight. Instead, he hunched over slightly, as though he were being pulled down by the weight of his own misery.

'Humbug!' he muttered to himself through his sharp lips, as his narrow eyes observed the prize turkey hanging in the butcher's window – for, as you have probably guessed, this miser of a man *hated Christmas*.

Actually, *hate* isn't a strong enough word for how he felt about Christmas. Let me look in the dictionary for a better one. Do you know any?

Let me see . . .

Disliked? Nope, still not strong enough.

Loathed? Not quite . . .

Detested? Getting better!

Resented? **Almost** . . .

The thing is, when it came to Christmas, this man felt **ALL** those words put together.

That's it! He *disloathesented* Christmas!

All right – that's a bit silly and made up. **BUT** there is one word in the dictionary that sums up this miserable man perfectly . . . and it just so happens to be his name:

SCROOGE!

Ebenezer Scrooge, to be precise.

Perhaps you've heard of him?

He's the sprout on your Christmas dinner plate. The coffee-flavoured disappointment in your box of chocolates. The pair of socks disguised as a present under the tree.

When it comes to *disloathesenting* Christmas, he's the **GOAT** (Grinchiest Of All Time), and if old Scrooge had his way, he'd get rid of Christmas altogether.

We don't need to worry, though. Ebenezer Scrooge is merely a character in a very famous old book called *A Christmas Carol*, by an author named Charles Dickens. *He's not real.*

Right?

Well, no. That's not quite true.

If you leave a book closed and unread, it's almost as if the people and places inside it don't exist at all. But once you open it up, and those words start to ping around someone's mind – like these ones are pinging around yours right now! –

those people are set free into the wilds of your imagination.

That is why we must be very careful as we step into the next part of this story together that we don't let anything step out . . .

Chapter One

THE HOLLY JOLLY JINGLERS

'*Fa-lala-lala, lala-la-la!*' sang Bob Trundle as he expertly lassoed the Christmas tree with a string of red tinsel like a Christmas cowboy.

You might recognize this merry scene! That's right – we're at the wonky little home of the Trundle family, the heroes of this story, and, as you can probably tell, they are getting ready for the big day.

'You're not redecorating the tree **AGAIN**, are you?' asked Pamela, handing him a cup of hot chocolate overflowing with marshmallows, just the way Bob liked it.

9

'Of course! There're exactly ten days until Christmas, and it needs to look fresh for the big day!' Bob said, taking a nice, sugary sip of warm chocolate before picking up another string of tinsel.

'Yes, I know, and I'm fully supportive of your unique Christmas decorating style, my dear, but I think there's probably more tinsel than there is tree!' she said, pointing at the flamboyant fir that seemed to be trembling under the impossible amount of tinsel and baubles balanced on every branch.

'If I've said it once, I've said it a hundred times,' Bob started. 'When it comes to Christmas trees . . .'

'You can never have enough tinsel!' cheered William, as he zoomed into the room with another shimmering string, throwing it on the branches as he did a lap of the Christmas tree.

'That's my boy. Just like his dad, eh!' Bob laughed, but that last piece of tinsel had barely settled when the tree creaked . . .

then crunched . . .

then collapsed completely . . .

CRASH!

. . . leaving behind a cloud of Christmassy sparkles.

'Not again!' Brenda sighed, as she joined the family in the living room. '*If I've said it once, I've said it a hundred times,*' she said in her best Bob voice. '*When it comes to Christmas trees . . .*'

'You can never use too much tinsel!' finished Pamela, winking at her daughter, who was carrying a large model of a building made out of ice-lolly sticks, yoghurt pots and cotton-wool balls.

'Wow! Your Christmas project is looking great!' Pamela said, admiring all the icicles made of glue and glitter (the environmentally friendly stuff, of course).

'Is that Santa's Snow Ranch?' William asked.

'Yeah! Take a look inside,' Brenda said, beaming with pride as she opened up her school project to reveal its sparkly, glittering interior.

'Awesome!' William smiled as he recognized all the magical places they'd been during their adventures with Santa and the Christmasaurus.

'Look, tiny Naughty and Nice Lists!' Bob cried.

'And a mini Christmasaurus!' William cheered, pointing to a shiny model dinosaur with a mane made of tinfoil icicles and covered in – you guessed it – *more glitter*!

'What's that amazing smell?' Pamela asked, leaning in and getting a good sniff.

'**CRUMPETS!**' the others chorused, as Brenda explained that her model snow ranch's kitchen walls were made of the elves' favourite toasted treat.

'That's the smallest Christmas tree I've ever seen!' said Bob, using his glasses as a magnifying glass to study the tiny tree.

'It might be small, but it's looking better than ours,' Pamela said, reminding Bob of the mess on the living-room floor.

'Not to worry! I'll be back in a jingle.' He ran to the hallway and dived into the cupboard under the stairs. A couple of crashes, a few bangs and a jingle of bells later, he returned with . . .

'The back-up tree!' he announced, dragging a fresh Christmas tree into the living room.

'How many Christmas trees have you got in there, Bob?' asked Pamela, raising an eyebrow.

'Oh, one or two.' Bob winked as he stood up, the new tree in place.

'We'll have to start calling you *Bob Back-Up-Tree Trundle*!' Pamela laughed as William set to work, helping his dad transfer decorations from the collapsed tree to the fresh one.

Now, you might already be able to tell that when it came to Christmas, Bob Trundle was the total opposite of that Scrooge fellow I told you about.

Bob was the pigs-in-blankets on your Christmas dinner plate, the triple-chocolate-fudge truffle with extra sprinkles in your box of chocolates, the surprise present you hadn't even asked for.

He was the anti-Scrooge – and his son, William, was a close second in command.

They **LOVED** everything about Christmas, and this year was doubly exciting for them. In fact, it was *double*-doubly exciting! Maybe even *double-double-doubly* exciting, and you're about to see why . . .

'We're all *double-double-doubly* excited to watch your first Christmas carol concert next week in the town square, William!' said Bob. 'I've got a feeling you're going to get chosen for the big solo, just like I did in my first year with the Holly Jolly Jinglers!'

Brenda giggled. 'The Holly Jolly *what*?'

'The Holly Jolly **JINGLERS**!' said Bob and William at the same time, as though it were jinglingly obvious.

'It's the name of the Holly Heath Primary School carolling choir,' explained Bob.

'And it's not any old carolling choir. They are the greatest Christmas carol singers in the whole country!' added William.

'And you used to be one of these *Holly . . . Jolly . . . Jingly* people?' Brenda asked Bob.

'Oh yes, of course! I was a HJJ back when I was your age. I was chosen for the solo, and in my very first year too!'

'What's so good about a solo? I think I'd rather hide at the back where no one can see what I'm up to,' Brenda whispered to William.

'Singing the solo is very special, Brenda. Nothing fills the heart with Christmas spirit quite like the angelic sound of a child singing a Christmas carol.' Bob paused for a moment to wipe a tear from his cheek with his best Christmas hanky. 'And I'd bet a hundred jingles that this year it'll be our Willypoos.'

'Really, Dad?' William said hopefully.

'Abso-jolly-lutely! I've seen *the signs*,' Bob said, waving his hands like he was sprinkling invisible magic in the air.

'What signs?' asked Brenda, one eyebrow raised, ready to not believe anything Bob was about to say.

Bob smiled and said, 'Well, when I woke up this morning there was a robin on my windowsill.'

'So?' Brenda shrugged.

'**SO**, it looked **JUST LIKE** the robin on my Christmas jumper the year I sang the solo! If that isn't a sign, I'll eat Santa's hat. You've got to read the signs, Willypoos, and I think they're all pointing at **YOU**!'

'I hope so, Dad!' William said, smiling. 'I've been practising loads!'

'Yeah, we know!' groaned Brenda. 'But if you could *not* practise at six in the morning, then I think all of us might be a bit jollier!'

'Oh, Brenda,' said Bob, laughing. 'There's never a bad time to practise being a Holy Jolly Jingler, especially if you want to sing a solo. Back when I was a HJJ, I'd be up at the crack of dawn, warming up these pipes for the solo audition.

'Fa-lala-la . . . '

As his dad sang, William felt a warm hand on his.

'William, you do know it doesn't matter if you get a solo or not,' said Pamela, smiling at him. 'Being in a choir is about singing *together* as a team, just like we'll all be there as a team to watch, solo or no solo!' she finished, and William noticed her give Bob one of those special looks that grown-ups do, which somehow seem to say something without actually saying anything at all.

The Holly Jolly Jinglers

'Oh . . . yes . . . you're right, er . . . of course. Solo or not, we'll be there in the town square, cheering you on!' Bob said, giving William a little wink when Pamela wasn't looking.

'Thanks, Dad,' replied William, but he couldn't help a note of sadness creeping into his voice.

'Everything all right? I thought you were excited about the carols?' Bob asked.

'Oh, I am! Only, if I *do* get the solo, it'll be a big moment for me, *really* big, and . . . well, having you all there will be great, but . . . I just wish *everyone* I care about could be there, that's all,' William said.

The whole family knew instantly who he was talking about.

Yes, I think *you've* probably guessed it too . . .

'Well, I'm sure there's a certain *blue dinosaur* who would very much like to be there as well,' Bob said gently.

'You've not written your letter to Santa yet. Why don't you include a note to invite the Christmasaurus?' Pamela suggested.

'Yes! Invite Santa too!' added Brenda.

William felt pride and excitement tingling through

him as he imagined taking centre stage on the bandstand in the middle of the town square, singing his heart out, with the most magical audience imaginable watching him: Santa (yes – the **REAL** Santa!), and his best friend in the whole world, the Christmasaurus (or as William sometimes called him – *Chrissy*). Almost immediately, the idea fizzled out in his mind and he shook his head. 'I don't know . . . They'll be snowed under with preparations for Christmas. They'd never be able to come to a silly carol concert on Christmas Eve!' he said.

'Silly?! Did you just call the Holly Jolly Jinglers *silly*?' Bob gasped.

'You know what I mean, Dad. They've got more important things to do this time of year.' William sighed.

'Everyone has time for friends at Christmas, William,' Bob said with a smile, pulling his favourite candy-cane-shaped pen from his pocket and handing it to his son.

William hesitated, then took the pen. 'I guess there's no harm in inviting them . . .'

So, while William set to work on his letter to Santa, let us take a little trip up north, **ALL** the way north, to see the big man himself. After all, it's page nineteen and we've not seen the star of this book yet. And not to worry – there's a blue dinosaur waiting in the next chapter . . .

CHAPTER TWO

THE NEXT CHAPTER

I'm sure you've got a pretty good idea of what the North Pole looks like.

You've seen it in the movies, heard the songs, read the books . . . Well, let me tell you again anyway, for even if you've seen it before a hundred squillion times, the North Pole is always completely mind-bogglingly awesome.

Imagine this: there wasn't a single cloud in the star-filled sky, yet snowflakes the size of marshmallows were falling.

Pretty magical, right?

That's not all. They tasted like marshmallows too!

(The white ones, not the pink ones.)

And this entirely cloudless, marshmallow-flavoured, snowflake-making sky was full of bluey-green light that was dancing – *actually* dancing. (I think it was a foxtrot.)

And to dance, you need music, of course, and there was **ALWAYS** music in the North Pole, thanks to the tiny singing elves. (We'll meet them in a moment.)

The snowmen weren't standing still like the ones in your garden, but skating around on Santa's frozen swimming pool (I don't know who thought it would be a good idea to build an outdoor pool in the Arctic!), and, overhead, reindeer were swooshing this way and that, testing out the aerodynamics of their antlers.

It was, without doubt, the most magical place that could ever exist, and in the centre of it all was the jolliest of people, a massive merry man with a beard whiter than snow and eyes like blue flames, wearing red with white trim from his head to his boots. Even the pair of giant fluffy earmuffs he wore over his ears were red.

'Ho, ho, ho!'

he boomed . . .

Well, what were you expecting him to say? It's Santa, after all!

'Here they come, here they come!' he said, giddily prancing around and pointing at something in the sky.

Pop!

A tiny elf appeared by his side, wearing a smart uniform with a satchel over her shoulder and a large net in her tiny hands. Her name was Sort.

Pop! Pop!

Two more elves appeared, wearing the same uniform. They were Staple and Stamp. They were carrying long sticks with smaller nets on the end, which looked like the sort of thing you might catch butterflies with.

Pop! Pop! Pop! Pop!

In an instant, Santa was surrounded by a whole team of elves carrying nets on long poles, and all in the same uniform with a very official-looking badge that said:

POOPS – Polar Operations Official Postal Service.

23

Each elf was staring up at the twinkling stars as though they were waiting for something to happen.

'Any second, any moment,
Catching elves, get ready!
Prepare your pickers, spread your nets
And hold your crumpets steady!'

Sort sang. Like all North Pole elves, the Polar Operations Official Postal Service staff only spoke in merry rhyme. (Yes, it does get annoying occasionally – just ask Santa.)

The POOPS elves took a synchronized crunch of their crumpets (an elf favourite) and put the rest in their crumpet pouches to save for later, because the stars overhead had stopped twinkling and were now flickering.

'Steady . . . steady . . .' instructed Santa, noticing this change in the sky.

The flicker gradually became a flutter.

'Not yet . . . !' Santa said, feeling the excitement from the elves around him build.

Then suddenly the stars weren't stars at all . . .

24

THE NEXT CHAPTER

They were *envelopes*! Thousands and thousands of them, flitting across the sky like a flock of birds, except birds fly south for the winter whereas these letters had all flown north!

'Here we go-ho-ho! Time to round up the first letters of the year, my elves!' And, with that, Santa blew a whistle, and the catching began.

The elves back-flipped and forward-flipped, swiping around the sky with their long letter-nets, scooping up letter after letter.

Another squad of elves opened up the bigger nets like huge parachutes and scooped up hundreds of wild letters at a time. **SWOOSH!**

Now, you may already know that the farming elves, who will be *dig, dig, diggedy digging* into the ice for toys very soon, sing a special digging song while they work . . . Well, these posty elves have a little song that they sing too.

Do you want to hear it?

Are you sure? Because once it's in your head it's very hard to get out. But if you insist . . .

All right! The tune is a bit like 'Jingle Bells' (but feel free to make up your own – it'll still be just as annoying):

A Christmasaurus Carol

'Letters here, letters there,
Letters in the air!
If we didn't catch them,
They would end up **EVERYWHERE!**

Oh! Letters here, letters there,
Letters in the sky!
Seems a little silly but
There's one good reason why. . .

There's a jolly man
Dressed head to toe in red.
(That includes his pants,
And the hat upon his head!)

The Next Chapter

At this time of year,
If you write a note to him,
He'll bring you anything you want
And that is why we sing . . .

Oh! Letters here, letters there,
Fly at lightning speed!
Listing lots of stuff that parents
Say their kids don't need!

Oh! Letters here, letters there,
Sent from girls and boys.
If they're nice, then Santa might
Just bring them lots of toys!'

These POOPS elves sang this over and over, like a broken record, until EVERY last letter was scooped out of the sky . . . which took HOURS!

(If you're wondering why Santa wore those red earmuffs during this letter-catching ceremony, it wasn't to keep his ears warm – it was to keep their singing out.)

OK, I know what you're all thinking. Santa's red pants, right?

BUT that's not all. You're also thinking, *You said there was going to be a dinosaur in the next chapter, and he's nowhere to be seen!*

Well, don't get your stockings in a twist, because hiding at the end of this very sentence, at the edge of the forest of Christmas trees, was one impossible blue creature called **THE CHRISTMASAURUS**.

There. Are you happy now?

As he hid among the prickly branches of the Christmas trees, watching letters falling from the stars, his eyes darted around, as though he were looking for one in particular.

SANTA

If you or I were to try to find one specific envelope in all those squillions of letters, it would be like finding an elephant in your bowl of cereal.

All right, I suppose *that* would actually be quite easy, but what I mean is that *this* would be *impossible*!

But the Christmasaurus wasn't you or me (unless you are the Christmasaurus reading this book, in which case, *Hello, Christmasaurus!).* The Christmasaurus could do impossible things because he was an impossible creature.

Firstly, he was a dinosaur, the only one alive – *impossible*! And he could fly without wings or antlers or propellers or pixie dust – *impossible*! **AND** he could sniff out William Trundle's letter as it fell like a shooting star – **IMPOSSIBLE**!

He leapt from his hiding place, launched into the sky and soared towards the plummeting piece of post. He caught it gently in his teeth and landed next to Santa, wagging his tail excitedly.

'What have you got there?' Santa chuckled as he took the envelope from the Christmasaurus and opened it up. 'Well, bless my Kringles, it's a letter from our friend William Trundle!'

The Christmasaurus let out a joyous roar.

'Yes, yes, I'll read it to you. Sit!' said Santa, and the Christmasaurus giddily plopped his blue bottom on the soft snow and listened to Santa read William's letter.

CHAPTER THREE

WILLIAM'S LETTER

Dear Santa and Chrissy,

How are you both? I can't believe it's December already. I bet you're getting excited for the big day. Although probably not half as excited as my dad. He's had all the decorations up since the moment Halloween ended. I know, that's actually super-late for Dad, who usually starts Christmas decorations in July, but it was a promise he made Pamela – no Christmas until Halloween is over!

Dad really struggled with that one but, to be honest, I quite enjoyed giving Halloween its moment this year instead of confusing trick-or-treaters with our holly wreath and fairy lights!

Don't worry, though – Christmas is still my favourite time of year.

Brenda managed to stay out of trouble this year, so you'll probably see her pop up on the Nice List again . . . well, apart from that time she 'accidentally' threw her Neverball (remember, the never-melting snowball that she wished for when we visited that magical forest of wishes with you . . . ?) through the garden-shed window, which meant that Pamela found Dad's secret stash of Christmas chocolates he'd been hiding in there. Most of them were just empty wrappers too!

But, overall, the four of us have really started to feel like a family! We even had our first family holiday to the beach.

Dad and Brenda made a sandman. . .
And Pamela and I made a Sandy-saurus.
Look familiar?

I hope you've had a relaxing year up
there at the North Pole. Have you been
getting much flying practice, Chrissy?

How are Snozzletrump, Specklehump, Sparklefoot, Sugarsnout, Starlump, Spudcheeks, Snowcrumb and Sprout?

I bet Spudcheeks and Snozzletrump will be toasting and buttering those crumpets right about now, and the others are probably dusting off their tools ready to dig, dig, diggedy dig for toys.

Oh, that reminds me!

I don't want any toys this year. I know that's a bit unusual. You're probably up to your beard with thousands of letters from other kids asking for all the toys under the Northern Lights, but there's something I want WAY more than any toy.

For Christmas this year, I just want to see you.

Well, actually, I would like YOU to come and see ME in my first-ever Christmas carol concert.

I'm singing with the Holly Jolly Jinglers in our town square. I think you'll like our style. We sing a lot of songs about you, Santa!

The only problem is, the concert is on Christmas Eve!

It's a big ask, and I know you're probably SUPER-busy, but if you do have a spare few minutes in between delivering presents around the world, then there's a nice little rooftop that overlooks the square that you could watch from. I've sent a flyer for the concert with this letter so you can see where and when.

It would mean the world to me, as I might even be singing my first solo! I've not actually been given a solo yet, but Dad seems to think it's going to happen and he was a Jingler himself (a LONG time ago!), so he knows his jingles.

Anyway, Brenda's here beside me. She says hi and that she definitely still wants presents this year and will be writing to you with a list soon.

Hope to see you at the concert!

Your friend,

WILLIAM TRUNDLE

A Christmasaurus Carol

Santa looked at the Christmasaurus, who was gazing back at him with big round eyes and his best cute puppy face. A face that said, *PLEASE, PLEASE,* **PLEASE** *can we go and watch William's carol concert?*

'Hmmmm, it's on Christmas Eve, so time will be tight . . .' Santa said, scratching his beard as he thought.

The Christmasaurus whimpered and nudged Santa with his cold snout.

Santa's beard twitched into a smile.

'There's always enough time for carols on Christmas Eve,' he said with a wink.

The Christmasaurus was so delighted he bounced into the air as if he'd sat on an icicle, before slumping into Santa's arms and slurping his face with a slobbery dino thank you.

On Christmas Eve, they would have the joy of watching William sing!

CHAPTER FOUR
JINGLERS, ASSEMBLE!

When the school bell rang for home time at Holly Heath Primary the next day, William shot out of the classroom faster than a flying reindeer and zoomed straight to the hall where it was time to join the Holly Jolly Jinglers for choir practice.

'Come in, come in! Take your positions. *Jinglers, assemble!*' trilled his music teacher, Miss Melody, as if she were forming some sort of festive superhero team.

'Ah yes, we have another Trundle joining the Jinglers this year,' Miss Melody said excitedly as she spotted William. 'I remember your father's first solo. He was quite the Jingler – I have high hopes for you!'

Miss Melody had been teaching music at the school for as long as the school existed. 'Eddie, my dear, will you please pass around the carol books?'

'Sure thing, Miss Melody,' chimed Eddie Shepherd, who was in his third year with the Holly Jolly Jinglers and was **SO** jingle-jolly he could have given Bob Trundle a run for his jingle bells. Eddie merrily skipped around the hall, handing out carol books before taking his favourite spot in the choir – front and centre.

The Holly Jolly Jinglers were now assembled in their positions and eager to sing.

'Let's warm up with something jolly! Turn to page ten. Let's get ready to jingle!' Miss Melody cried enthusiastically, and the Holly Jolly Jinglers flicked through their carol books.

William did too, even though he knew the words to every Christmas carol off by heart, upside down, back to front, fast or slow and every which way in between. He could literally sing them all backwards if you asked him to.

Seriously! You should hear him sing 'Elgnij Slleb'!

Miss Melody began tinkling away at the piano as the Jinglers took a deep breath and started to sing.

Jinglers, Assemble!

Except this wasn't just any singing. The hall filled up instantly with Christmas spirit, as if someone had turned on the tap and let festive cheer flow into the room. Their voices echoed up and down the school corridors, and anywhere their singing could be heard became a more cheerful place.

'Wonderful!' Miss Melody applauded. 'And splendid high notes from you as usual, Eddie.'

'Thank you, miss.' Eddie smiled and gave a little bow.

'Are we all feeling Christmassy?' asked Miss Melody, and all the Jinglers cheered.

'Of course you are! Who can tell me why?'

William put his hand in the air, but Eddie in the front and centre beat him to it.

'Because Christmas carols aren't like ordinary songs. Carols are magic! It's impossible for anyone to hear one and not feel Christmassy,' he said, sounding almost as chirpy as a North Pole elf.

Eddie was right, of course! There's something special about Christmas carols that does seem a little bit magical. Whenever you hear one, no matter the time of year, it'll make you feel that little jingle of Christmassy warmth. It could be the end of July in the summer holidays, but a little snippet of a carol will transport you straight to December and fill you with merriness.

Try it for yourself!

Sing a little Christmas song right now. Any one you want.

Go on.

I'll wait . . .

Seriously, the story will still be here when you're done.

All finished?

I bet you're feeling more Christmassy than you were before, aren't you? See! That's the magic of a Christmas carol.

'Next page!' Miss Melody instructed, and the Jinglers flicked through their books and began singing 'Deck the Halls'.

A little *fa-lala-la* later, they harmonized their way through 'Hark the Herald Angels Sing', then amazed Miss Melody with 'Away in a Manger' before crooning 'O Christmas Tree'.

Jinglers, Assemble!

After each song, Miss Melody beamed with jolliness and called out things like: 'Beautiful vibrato, *Eddie*!' and 'Can you all try to sing as loudly as *Eddie* next time!' or 'That's how it's done, *Eddie*!'

Now, I'm not saying anything bad about Eddie. He was a nice enough kid who did nicely at school, had a very nice voice and was, well . . . *Nice List* material.

And I'm not saying anything bad about Miss Melody either. She's a teacher, after all, and you should always remember to say nice things about the people who mark your work.

But Miss Melody was so used to saying nice things about Eddie that she was like a broken record, stuck saying them on repeat.

I'll let you into a little secret. If you hear something said enough times, over and over again, your brain will start to believe it – even if it isn't completely true.

So, by this point, Eddie believed he was the Jolliest Jingler that ever lived on Planet Jingle, and that no one else stood a chance of out-jingling him – but the problem was that William was now starting to believe it too. And so, instead of proudly booming out carols, he slouched in his wheelchair and made himself small and unnoticeable.

'Jinglers, the time has come! Turn to page seven!' Miss Melody said dramatically, and the Holly Jolly Jinglers started whispering with excitement. They all knew that page seven in the choir book was *THE song* – the song that one lucky Jingler would be selected to sing solo!

'Let's sing it once together,' said Miss Melody, and, as she played the piano, the Jinglers sang:

> 'Once upon a Christmas,
> In a little town,
> No fairy lights were glowing
> And people wore a frown.
>
> But then it started snowing
> And a child began to sing,
> Spreading Christmas joy
> To everyone and everything.
>
> Lighting up the night,
> Candles shining bright,

Jinglers, Assemble!

A Christmas carol
Will fill the world with light.

At this time of year,
Any time you hear
A Christmas carol,
You will feel the Christmas cheer.'

As they finished, there was a short moment of Christmassy calmness before Miss Melody cleared her throat.

'Any Jinglers who think they have what it takes to sing that solo, raise your hand,' Miss Melody said, making the solo sound so incredibly important that it almost felt as though Christmas itself might depend on it.

'*Solo* . . .' William whispered to himself nervously.

This was it – the moment he had been waiting for. All he had to do was put his hand up. But . . . he *couldn't*!

He knew he *should* put it up. He *wanted* to put it up! But there was this little voice in the back of his brain saying:

Do you really want to sing the solo?

In front of the whole town?

What if everyone laughs?
What if people say you're rubbish?

By the time his brain had stopped saying stuff like that, there were four hands in the air, volunteering for the solo: Marcus Grimble, Grace Hobbs, Kai Singh and, of course, Eddie Shepherd.

'Marcus Grimble, let's hear you first,' called Miss Melody. Marcus nervously took a swig from a bottle of fizzy drink to clear his throat.

'Come along, Marcus – we haven't got all day!' Miss Melody snapped, and with a wave of her hand he began singing:

'Once upon a Christmas . . . '

Marcus stopped singing as his tummy made a great gurgling sound before a deep, fizzy belch blasted out of his mouth . . .

BUUUURP!

44

Jinglers, Assemble!

'Charming. How very Christmassy,' Miss Melody said sarcastically. 'It's a *no* this year, Marcus.' She smiled, like she was a judge on *Holly Heath's Got Talent*, and poor Marcus seemed to deflate like a balloon.

'Grace Hobbs, when you're ready . . .'

Grace took a deep breath and gave it her best shot.

'Once upon a Christmas,
In a little town,
No fairy lights were . . . were . . .'

Flustered, Grace stopped singing. The words had just flown out of her brain like one of Santa's reindeer!

'Oh dear, oh dear,' tutted Miss Melody. 'Rule number four of the Jinglers' code: *a Jingler must remember their lyrics.*'

Grace went as red as Santa's hat and stepped back in line.

'Kai Singh, can *you* remember the words?' Miss Melody said.

'Once upon a Christmas,
In a . . . A . . . ATCHOOOO!'

A sneeze erupted from Kai like a very merry volcano!

'Sorry, miss – I'm allergic to Christmas trees!' Kai said, pointing to the school tree in the corner of the hall.

'Bless you, Kai. Perhaps you would be more suited to joining the summer choir, *the Sweaty Singers*,' Miss Melody suggested.

That left only *one* person with their hand in the air.

'Eddie Shepherd.' Miss Melody beamed at him. 'I hardly need to ask you to sing, but it's always such a joy. Why don't you treat us all?'

Eddie stepped forward and sang the most perfect solo William had ever heard. It was as though someone had decorated his eardrums for Christmas, and when Eddie finished, the whole choir exploded with applause.

'Oh my! That might just be the best Jingling solo we've had since Bob Trundle. Oh yes, that reminds me . . .' Miss Melody clapped, calling for everyone to calm down. 'Is there anyone else who wants to give it a try?' She looked straight at William.

This was it – the moment William had been waiting for! But instead of confidently taking centre stage and singing his heart out like he'd planned, William would have preferred a trapdoor to open in the stage floor that he could escape into. He wondered if his wheelchair had a secret invisibility button on it – or perhaps if he wished hard enough, the Christmasaurus would burst through the roof and fly him out of there. ANYTHING to get him out of singing on his own!

It didn't matter how much William wanted that solo, or how much he hoped to make his dad proud – when Miss Melody's eyes looked into his, he found himself nervously shaking his head.

NO WAY!

'Very well then. It's decided. This year, it will be Eddie singing the solo!' Miss Melody announced, just as the bell rang and choir practice was over.

William left the hall feeling as blue as the Christmasaurus's bottom as that voice in his brain piped up once again with: *How are you going to tell Dad?*

CHAPTER FIVE

BEJINGLED

William and Brenda were old enough to make their way home from school by themselves these days, as long as they stayed together. Although it was dark and cold after school at this time of year, William loved the Christmassy journey across town . . . Well, he usually did, but after that choir practice he wasn't feeling very merry at all. In fact, despite the deep snow on the ground and snowmen in front gardens, William was feeling about as unmerry as a person could get!

'What's up with you?' asked Brenda, who was waiting for him outside the school gates.

'Nothing,' William said, harrumphing.

'*Nothing?* Then why does your face look like you just chewed a soggy sprout?' Brenda asked playfully, but William wheeled himself straight past her without saying a word.

'Hey!' called Brenda. 'I had to wait an hour to walk home with you.'

'I didn't ask you to,' William muttered.

'I know, but it's called *being nice*. Remember? That thing you're always trying to get me to be?' She smiled, giving him a little nudge to try to snap him out of his grump, but William didn't reply. Instead, they headed across town in silence.

Finally, Brenda couldn't bear it.

'Blimey, what's turned you into such a *grumpy bum*?!' She laughed, trying to lift the mood.

'I'm not,' William insisted.

'You're right. Actually, you're a moody sprout-lump,' Brenda teased.

William huffed. 'No, I'm not!'

'OK. You're a *huffy-stropkins* . . . *a grizzly turnip* . . . a **GROTTY SNOT-BAG**!'

William slammed on his brakes and skidded his

wheelchair to a stop in the middle of the snowy path.

There was silence.

'If you're not going to tell me what's wrong, I might as well walk home alone,' Brenda said.

'Maybe you should,' William fired back, knowing full well that was forbidden.

What he'd forgotten, though, was that as much as she was trying to stay out of trouble these days, deep down Brenda was allergic to following rules. Any opportunity she came across to ignore them, you can bet your last Christmas cracker she'd take it!

'Fine. If that's what *you* want, I will,' Brenda said.

'Fine!'

'FINE!'

And with a swish of her blonde curls, Brenda walked away, leaving William all alone.

Of course, William felt bad instantly. Brenda hadn't deserved him snapping at her and, if he was being honest with himself, he knew he was totally being a moody sprout-lump AND a huffy-stropkins, and definitely a grizzly turnip too.

William wasn't upset with Eddie for getting the solo

either. He was an awesome singer and totally deserved it. And he wasn't annoyed with Miss Melody. She had chosen the best person who had auditioned, after all.

So, if he wasn't upset with Brenda or Eddie or Miss Melody, who was he upset with, I wonder?

You guessed it. He was upset with *himself*.

Why?

For not even *trying* for the solo!

And why did he feel so bad?

Well, it's easy being annoyed with others, but being annoyed with *yourself* is one of the toughest things in life.

The final echoes of Brenda's footsteps disappeared, and William was alone on the street now – but he didn't feel alone, because there were little voices gossiping in his head, saying things like . . .

I can't believe he didn't put his hand up for the solo.

Then another one chimed in . . .

It wouldn't have made any difference!
He's not good enough to sing solo anyway!

Then both of them said . . .

How's he going to tell his jolly-jingling dad that he didn't even try to get the solo?

And worst of all . . .

I suppose he'll have to write to Santa and the Christmasaurus and tell them not to bother showing up to the concert.
He wouldn't want to waste their time . . .

With so much noise in his noggin, William wasn't ready to go home. He decided to take the long route back to their wonky little house, along one of the most Christmassy streets he knew, right on the edge of town, where Holly Heath ends and the next town, Whiffington, begins.

It was always extra Christmassy here thanks to a little festive rivalry between the two neighbouring towns. On one side of the street were the Holly Heath houses (who always had far brighter decorations – in William's opinion!) and on the other were the Whiffington's.

He passed Mr Ridley's place with his reindeer decorations and plastic singing Christmas tree in the driveway, then Mrs Jones's, a few doors down, who had two snowmen dancing on the garage roof, and not forgetting the Cawleys in the big house at the end, whose front garden was overflowing with light-up elves.

On any ordinary day, William wouldn't have been able to take his eyes off these glowing houses. It would have been like he'd been hypnotized . . . bewitched . . .

bejingled!

But not today.

Today he didn't want to look at them at all. Each decoration, every flashing elf, every singing Christmas tree and dancing snowman reminded him of the carol concert.

For the first time in his life, William wished that Christmas . . . He wished that it would . . .

Oh, I don't even want to write it, so I'll let William say it himself.

'I wish Christmas would just GO AWAY!' he shouted.

At the exact moment those words left his lips, everything went quiet.

BEJINGLED

Mr Ridley's tree wasn't singing any more. Mrs Jones's snowmen had stopped pirouetting on the garage roof. The Cawleys' elves weren't twinkling on their lawn, and the sign in the window of the mysterious library said: *OPEN* . . .

WAIT!

Mysterious library?

Where did that come from?!

'I've never seen that library before,' whispered William to himself, looking at the strange little building that had somehow managed to stay hidden from him for his whole life.

It was a thin brick building that seemed to be wedged in between two houses, like that last book you somehow manage to squeeze on to your bookshelf even though it doesn't really fit.

Over the door, the name of the library was painted on a weathered sign: **The Night-Before Library**.

William read the name out loud and, as though he'd uttered some sort of magic password, the library replied with . . .

DING-A-LING!

An old bell rang as the door to the library swung open with a long *creeeEAAK*! Even though no one had come in or out.

Spooky, right?

I don't know about you, but if I were William, I would have whizzed straight home and never looked back. That wouldn't make a very good story, though, so instead William called out, 'Hello?'

There was a pause.

Suddenly William noticed a sign on the door, half covered with snow. At least it was, until a gust of wind blew in from the north and cleared away the snow, revealing two words – **COME IN!**

A shiver went down William's spine, and those nagging voices in his head were replaced by a memory of his dad saying, *'You've got to read the signs . . .'*

Well, this sign was about as clear as a snowball hitting you on the nose, so William wheeled his chair towards the open front door.

I bet you're yelling, '*NO,* **WILLIAM** *– this is so obviously a bad idea!*'

But unfortunately William can't hear you, or if he can, he's obviously decided to totally ignore you.

He disappeared inside the mysterious library just as the icy wind picked up once more, revealing one more word, which William hadn't read . . .

Oh dear.

It was too late.

CHAPTER SIX

THE NIGHT-BEFORE LIBRARY

*D*ING-A-LING!

The bell rang again as the door creaked shut behind William, sealing him inside the mysterious library, which had just appeared out of thin air.

If you thought that a library appearing out of nowhere was a bit strange, then wait until you hear about the *inside*. It was like no library William had ever seen before, and felt more like a sweetshop.

Past a wooden counter by the door, the shelves were overflowing with delicious feasts of fiction in every flavour imaginable, from plump paperbacks with peppermint-green pages to hardbacks with covers the colour of a cooked Christmas ham.

Fresh books shot through glass pipes that ran around the walls and twisted down the bookshelves, delivering them to the New Releases section. From the other side of the library came the comforting whiff of well-read vintage pages, wafting up William's nostrils.

It was magical!

'Wow!' William gasped in amazement as another fresh release zoomed across the room through a glass pipe, drawing his eye to some writing that was carved into the wooden bookshelves. It said:

Feel free to take a look,
But be warned, if you do,
In here you do not choose the book,
The book will choose you.

Before William had a chance to figure out what on earth that meant, there was a dull *thud* from somewhere towards the back of the library.

'Hello?' William called.

This was a library, after all. Surely somebody must work here.

He moved deeper into the forest of books in the direction of the *thud*, gazing up at the impossibly tall bookshelves towering above him. From the outside, the library had seemed tiny, but now that he was inside, it seemed to go on forever.

THUD!

He heard it again. Louder this time.

'Hello? Is anybody there?' he called, but again no one replied.

He approached the end of the row of shelves and was about to turn round when something caught his eye. Something out of place – it was a book, lying on the floor.

William scooped it up and turned it over in his hands.

The cover was deep ivy-green, and golden foil lettering on the front spelled out three words.

'*A Christmas Carol*,' William whispered to himself.

The library lights flickered like candles in a breath of wind.

It was then that William realized how unusually heavy

the book felt. At least twice as heavy as the one you're holding right now, but only around half as thick. Almost as though there had to be more inside it than just pages of paper.

It looked old too. *Really* old. The edges were worn and the pages looked like biscuits that had been dunked in tea.

Of course, William knew the story as well as anyone. *A Christmas Carol* was one of his dad's favourite books to read to him at Christmas (and any time of year, for that matter!).

But why was it on the floor?

William looked at the bookshelves around him and spotted a gap where one book was clearly missing.

It must have fallen off the shelf, he thought, and he slid it back into place where it fitted perfectly, like the final piece in a jigsaw puzzle.

SWOOSH!

Another book shot through the pipe overhead, making William jump.

'Brenda is going to love this place,' said William, chuckling to himself.

THE NIGHT-BEFORE LIBRARY

Brenda.

He sighed, suddenly remembering their silly argument. All the fun of a mysterious library had lifted his spirits for a while, but now he knew it was time to go and apologize. He was hoping that maybe the news of a secret library would make up for him being a complete grizzly turnip.

He wound his way to the front of the library, still hardly able to believe it existed at all, when suddenly a feeling washed over him. The feeling that he wasn't alone . . .

'Did you find everything you needed?' said a soft voice, floating from someone sitting behind the counter with their face buried deep in the pages of a book.

They startled William so much he nearly fell out of his chair! Had they been there this whole time? William was sure there had been no one sitting there when he entered.

'Didn't mean to scare you, dearie. I'm the librarian,' said the kind voice, the owner's face still hidden. 'Only, I wondered if you wanted to borrow that book.'

'What book?' William asked.

'The book on your lap,' the librarian said.

'There isn't a book on my –'

William suddenly felt it. The familiar weight of the book he'd just placed back on the shelf.

He looked down and, to his amazement, there *it* was. The ivy-green copy of *A Christmas Carol*, right there on his lap.

'How on earth did that get there?' William wondered aloud. 'I was sure I'd put that back.'

'Oh, it's hard to put a good book down.' The librarian chuckled as William placed it on the counter, firmly.

'I've already read this one. Well, my dad read it to me. He's a great storyteller,' William explained.

'Is he now?' the librarian said, their face still behind the book they were reading.

'Oh yes, he can really bring a story to life!'

A deep silence instantly flooded the library, and the lights flickered like candles once again.

'He brings them to life, does he?' the librarian whispered, and William couldn't help but notice the slight nervous tremble of the book in their hands.

William nodded.

'Then he should be very careful about what he chooses to read,' the librarian warned, peeling one hand from the spine of the book they were reading and placing it firmly on top of the copy of *A Christmas Carol*.

William laughed.

The librarian did not.

'Why is this place called the Night-Before Library? The night before *what?*' William asked.

The librarian lowered their book just enough for their twinkly eyes to peer through their reading spectacles and silently observe William.

Before William had his answer, a clock on the library wall chimed.

'Six o'clock! I'm afraid the Night-Before Library is closing now,' the librarian said.

DING-A-LING! The bell over the exit rang behind William and he spun to see the door swing open, inviting him to leave.

'Are you open tomorrow? I'd love to bring my sister . . .'

But when William turned round, the librarian had vanished, along with the copy of *A Christmas Carol*.

CHAPTER SEVEN
STORY TIME

William had left the library feeling a billion times less grizzly and grumpy than before he went in.

As he headed home, William wondered if there might be something special about libraries: something good for the soul. Any place you can wander in feeling like Clark Kent and fly out feeling like Superman must surely be magical.

William was so full of happy library thoughts as he wheeled down the path to his wonderfully wonky home that he didn't even notice his dad waiting in the doorway until he had practically rolled over his feet!

'Where have you been?' Bob barked, and behind his dad's back William caught a glimpse of Brenda poking her tongue out at him.

It was then that William knew he was in trouble. **BIG** trouble.

What William *didn't* know was that getting told off by his dad was going to be the least of his worries, because there was something else he hadn't noticed. A corner of deep ivy-green and a flash of gold peeped out of the seat pocket of his wheelchair . . .

'You know the rules, William. You and Brenda are only allowed to come home **TOGETHER**!' Bob said as William sheepishly stared at his feet . . . then his wheels . . . then the floor . . . *Anywhere* but at his dad,

who William could sense without even looking was wearing that *disappointed parent frown*, which always made him feel about as small as an elf.

'Anything could have happened to you, William! Didn't getting chased by a maniacal hunter a few years ago teach you anything?' said Pamela, who had joined Bob. She was more worried than angry, which didn't make William feel any better.

'You put yourself in danger and, what's worse, you put Brenda in danger too,' Bob said, nodding at Brenda, who was watching William get told off from the doorway with a mixture of guilt and delight.

William wished he could say *'She started it!'* like he normally did (because it was usually true). But this time . . . this time he was to blame. If there were one thing William had learnt from Brenda's many moments of mischief over the years, it was that when you've got yourself into a pickle, the quickest way out of it is to say . . .

'I'm sorry,' he said in his most *sorry*-sounding voice.

It was amazing how quickly those two words worked their magic. As Bob's frown faded, Brenda gave William a look that said, *Hey, that's my trick!*

'Well . . . all right . . . So, how did it go then?' Bob said, rubbing his hands together excitedly.

'How did what go?' William asked, moving towards the living room.

'Choir practice, of course!' said Bob, laughing.

In all the thrill of discovering a mysterious, hidden library, and then the disappointment and guilt of the telling-off once he'd got home, William had almost forgotten about the Holly Jolly Jinglers and that solo!

You know – the one he *didn't* get . . .

'Go on! Don't keep us waiting any longer!' Bob squeaked. 'We're desperate to hear if you got the solo!'

'Dad, I . . .' William started, his gaze meeting his dad's hopeful eyes.

This was when he was meant to tell everyone that he *didn't* get the solo. This was when he should have admitted that he'd felt too nervous to put his hand up.

This was his chance to be honest and say that he wasn't ready this year.

This was when William *didn't* do any of those things.

'I . . . GOT THE SOLO!' William lied.

Bob went crackers. In fact, he went absolutely

CHRISTMAS CRACKERS!

He started leaping around the room, cheering and whooping.

'I knew it! Just like his dad. You're a *Jingler* through and through!' Bob cried, hugging everyone in turn, and William tightest of all.

Over his dad's shoulder, William saw Brenda looking at him with her eyebrow raised. William might have fooled his dad and Pamela, but Brenda could sniff the whiff of a lie from a mile away, like a shark detecting a drop of blood in the ocean.

'What took you so long, anyway?' Brenda said, with narrow, suspicious eyes. 'I've been home for ages!'

'The library!' William blurted, grabbing the chance to change the subject from the choir.

'The *library*? But that's all the way on the other side of town!' Pamela said.

'No, I found a new library! Well, it's not *new* – it's actually kind of old. It's just down the road, next to Mr Ridley's house,' William said.

'I didn't know there was a library there. Did you, darling?' Pamela asked Bob, who was still beaming about the solo.

'I'd never seen it before either!' William explained. 'I was looking at the Christmas decorations on the houses . . .' He decided not to mention the part when he'd wished it would *all go away*, or his dad might faint. 'Then, next thing I knew, the library was just *there*, in between the houses! Like it had appeared out of nowhere! Oh, and you should see the inside. It was HUGE, and there were swirling glass pipes that zoomed books around over my head, and the smell of the pages was so delicious you could almost eat them. It was magical!'

'Oh, come on!' Brenda said, throwing her arms in the air. 'Mum, you're not going to believe that, are you? *A secret magic library, appearing out of nowhere!* Where did you *really* go?'

'The library! It's true!' William said.

'Prove it!' Brenda shouted.

THUD!

They all heard it.

The dull *donk* of an object hitting the floor just behind William's wheelchair.

'What's this?' Bob said, picking up something green.

Something that William recognized instantly.

'*That's impossible!*' William gasped as the familiar golden letters reflected the light.

'*A Christmas Carol.* Oh, this is one of my all-time favourites!' Bob said.

'Really? But isn't it a story about someone who hates Christmas?' Pamela asked.

'He doesn't just hate it – Scrooge wishes Christmas didn't exist at all! Not to worry, though, as he eventually learns that Christmas is the most wonderful time of the year. And what a beautiful edition,' Bob said, admiring the book in his hands.

'I thought I put that back on the counter,' William whispered to himself.

'Well, it looks like William was telling the truth about that library, doesn't it, *Brenda*?' Pamela nudged her daughter.

'Yeah. I suppose so. Sorry,' Brenda huffed, but William wasn't bothered about apologies. He was too busy trying to figure out just how that copy of *A Christmas Carol* had ended up in his house.

'Well, I can't think of a better book to read at this time of year. Story time?' said Bob with a grin.

STORY TIME

William and Brenda looked at each other with a little glint of excitement in their eyes. Neither of them could resist a Bob Trundle story time!

They all went to William's room, and Bob drew the curtains, dimmed the lights to set the mood and threw pillows on the floor. Brenda and William took their front-row positions as Pamela plonked a deep tin of delicious Christmas biscuits between them. 'Story snacks,' she said with a smile, before stealing her favourite shortbread and making herself comfortable.

'Settle down, settle down,' said Bob, calling for silence as he opened the ivy-green cover, turned to the first page and began bringing the story to life.

William's room became Bob's stage, and he had a knack for turning ordinary objects into props. He wrapped a curtain round his shoulders and it became Scrooge's coat. Bob's candy-cane-striped litter-picker, which he used to pick up wrapping paper on Christmas morning, was now Scrooge's cane. Next, he emptied the biscuits on to a plate and perched the tin on his head as Scrooge's top hat. Finally, he repositioned the bedside lamp, grabbed a few small objects close to hand

and arranged them so the shadows they cast on the wall looked like buildings, transforming the bedroom into the streets of Dickensian London.

Bob could play every character from the book perfectly too. William had watched this one-man show over many Christmases. One minute his dad was Scrooge, then Marley (he's a ghost . . . don't worry, he was dead to begin with), then the ghosts of Christmas past, present and future. Bob could become them all!

When Bob was reading to them, William, Brenda and Pamela didn't feel like they were in William's bedroom any more. It was as though they had been transported into the story. They all dreaded the moment when Bob would eventually say: 'That's all for tonight. Time for bed!'

But eventually he did.

'You can't stop there! It's just getting to the really good parts with the ghosts!' William whined.

'Yeah, Scrooge is still all *Scroogey*! You can't leave him like that,' Brenda added.

Bob smiled. 'Well, Scrooge will just have to stay Scroogey for one more night. We'll save him tomorrow!'

Story Time

They all said their goodnights and got ready for bed, but William couldn't sleep. Sometimes his dad's storytelling was so wonderfully real that the story carried on living in William's imagination long after Bob had put the book down.

It was like a movie playing over and over in his mind . . .

Scrooge crunching through the frosty streets, bah-humbugging humbugs into the cold night at the sight of anything remotely Christmassy.

Disloathesenting the very existence of all that was merry and bright.

Wishing it would all just disappear forever.

Just like I did earlier, William realized a little guiltily, before shaking the thought away and drifting off into a restless sleep full of strange dreams about Scrooge, though none of them were half as strange as what was soon to come.

CHAPTER EIGHT

A DECEMBER DISTURBANCE

Do you have a pet?

Has it ever stared into space, as if it could see something . . . or even *someone* you couldn't see?

Have you ever seen a dog bark at thin air, or a cat's fur go all sticky-uppy?

How about an animal in a deep, happy sleep, having a nice, warm dream about fluffy things and yummy stuff, then **BAM** – it's awake, sensing danger and ready to pounce?

Well, at the very same moment as William was

drifting off to sleep, hundreds of snowy miles away, in the warm reading room of Santa's Snow Ranch, *that's* exactly what happened to the Christmasaurus.

First, his scales twitched, then his nose itched, and finally **BAM** – the blue dinosaur was wide awake, leaping to his claws, his icy scales all sticky-uppy, his heart beating like galloping reindeer hooves in his chest.

'What is it, Chrissy?' Santa said, looking up from the Nice List as the Christmasaurus let out a low growl at something . . . someone that Santa couldn't see.

'*Danger?* Where?' Santa chuckled. 'My dear dino, you should know by now that you're always safe in the North P–'

Santa's beard twitched.

The Christmasaurus growled again.

'Yes, I sensed it that time too,' Santa whispered.

The Christmasaurus rippled his frosty scales and Santa twitched his beard once more, both scanning the air for signs of something wrong.

Suddenly they both felt it again.

It was bad. It was very bad.

'Outside.'

They both nodded , then Santa threw on his coat and slid into his heated slippers, and they headed out into the snowy night.

The Christmasaurus walked carefully and cautiously by Santa's side, staring into the shadows of the Christmas tree forest that surrounded them.

'Blinking **BAUBLES**, look up there!' Santa gasped, stopping in his tracks and gawping at the sky where the letters to Santa had arrived just a day earlier, and where the Northern Lights were now putting on their show.

At first glance, they were flowing as they always did, like enormous ocean waves over Santa's head, sending columns of green and purple light up towards the stars – but something wasn't right.

'Can you see it, Chrissy? The crack?' Santa said, pointing his gloved hand to the sky.

In the middle of the humungous waves of light, there was a thin black line running through them, like someone had taken an eraser on the end of a pencil and rubbed it across the sky, starting high above their heads and continuing all the way down to the horizon.

'A disturbance in the December sky is never a good sign,' Santa said, and the Christmasaurus whimpered.

'We must be ready . . .' Santa murmured.

The Christmasaurus let out a little, worried roar, as if to ask, *Ready for what?*

Santa took a deep breath before replying.

'Ready for trouble.'

CHAPTER NINE

CHRISTMESS

'WAKE UP! WAKE UP!' Brenda shrieked, loud enough to wake up the entire solar system.

William heard the crash and clatter of Bob and Pamela leaping out of bed and scuffling around, panicked footsteps clonking on the floor above, and their muffled voices talking to each other.

He checked the dinosaur-shaped clock on his bedside table. It was only six thirty in the morning, and – unless he'd accidentally slept for several days and today was actually Christmas Day – the fact that Brenda was awake before him meant only one thing. *Trouble!*

'What's the matter, Brenda?' Bob called as he and Pamela thundered down the hall towards Brenda's voice.

'Come quickly! The living room! I think we've been **BURGLED**!' Brenda cried.

William scrambled out of bed and into his wheelchair at Christmas-morning speed. He was in the living room with the rest of the family before you could say '*Jingle bells, Batman smells.*'

The room was a wreck!

Totally trashed from top to bottom.

It looked like someone had tipped the room upside down, put it in a washing machine on fast spin, then put that washing machine on a bouncy castle, which was loaded on to a truck that was driven over speedbumps during an earthquake.

Twice.

'We've been burgled, all right. Just look at the state of this place,' Pamela gasped, stepping into the wreck that used to be their living room.

'I don't believe it! I'd better phone the police!' Bob said.

William gazed around the room. What had been taken? There was the sofa with its three fat, comfy cushions. There was the cuckoo clock that William's granny had left them. There was Pamela's favourite pot plant, the fluffy rug with the chewed corners, thanks to their dog, Growler, the photographs of the four of them together . . .

Wait!

'Hang on, Dad,' William said. 'If we've been burgled, what did they steal?'

Bob, Pamela and Brenda all looked around the room again too.

'You're right, William!' exclaimed Bob.

'The TV's here!' cheered Brenda, throwing her arms round the telly and kissing the screen.

'So is my computer! Right where I left it,' said Pamela, picking up her untouched laptop. 'This would have been easy for a burglar to steal.'

'And they left the bobble hat I've been knitting! What kind of thief would leave that behind?' Bob asked.

'Everything is still here, right where it should be,' Pamela said.

But it wasn't. Not quite everything.

William gazed around once more.

'Everything except for the *Christmas decorations*,' he said.

There was a moment of silence. Then Bob fell to his knees as he realized that William was right. The mess in the room was entirely made up of his wonderful decorations.

'It's a Christ*mess*,' wailed Bob.

And it was. Just picture this . . .

* *The baubles were nothing more than piles of glittery dust on the floor.*
* *The strings of tinsel had become just plain old string.*
* *Each fairy light looked as though it had been individually stomped on.*
* *The star that once sat on top of the tree was now on the floor and completely pointless (literally).*
* *The Christmas tree itself had been stuffed up the chimney, so that only the base was sticking out, and the worst thing of all . . .*

'Not the Advent calendars!' Bob gasped as William picked up a squashed cardboard box that used to be his

Advent calendar and turned it round to reveal that all the doors had been opened and . . . (brace yourself)

...ALL THE CHOCOLATES HAD BEEN EATEN!

'There's more out here too!' Brenda said as she followed the festive destruction to the open front door, revealing their holly wreath sticking out of the wheelie bin.

'This is a disgrace. This is a disaster!' said Bob as he paced around, not knowing what to do with himself.

'Calm down, honey. Calm down,' Pamela said.

'*Calm down? Calm down?* How can I calm down when we've been the victim of an anti-Christmas crime!' Bob spluttered.

'Who would have broken into our house, trashed all the Christmas stuff, but not stolen anything?' William wondered out loud.

'A monster, that's who!' Bob wailed.

'Let's not be overdramatic. I'm sure there's a perfectly simple explanation,' Pamela said.

'Well, who do you think did this then?' Bob asked, with his eyebrows raised.

Pamela looked around, searching for clues – then suddenly snapped her fingers.

'A fox!' Pamela beamed.

'A *fox*?' Bob asked, pausing his pacing to consider it.

'Yeah!' Brenda said. 'We're learning about them at school. They get into houses all the time!'

William had to admit, it sounded possible. 'It could have squeezed in through Growler's dog-flap and didn't know how to get back out!' he suggested, and Growler barked his disapproval.

'So it panicked and started destroying everything in sight!' Pamela said with a satisfied smile, like she'd just solved a crime.

'That explains why nothing's missing,' Bob said thoughtfully.

'And why there's such a mess! Foxes are wild animals, after all, and don't like feeling trapped.' Brenda recited this fact from school.

Everyone stared at Bob, waiting for his verdict.

'Of course, it must have been a fox!' he cried. 'It's the only explanation. Phew! For a moment I thought we had some sort of Christmas-destroying monster on the loose!'

'Well, now that's settled, you two had better get yourselves ready for the last day of term while your father and I clean up this mess,' Pamela said.

'First things first. Back-up tree number two, here we come!' Bob Back-Up-Tree Trundle said as he rolled up his sleeves and marched to the cupboard under the stairs to dig out *another* Christmas tree from his seemingly endless supply.

William and Brenda, wanting to avoid having to clean up any mess, quickly got their uniforms on, said their goodbyes and headed to school.

'Well, that was a wild morning!' Brenda said as they followed their usual route to school past the same old houses.

'I know! When I heard you shouting **"WAKE UP!"** I thought, *Here we go again – why can't we just have an ordinary Christmas?*' William laughed, only to find that Brenda wasn't walking next to him.

He turned and saw that she'd stopped in the middle of the street.

'Brenda? We're only halfway to school – what's wrong?' William asked. 'You look like you've seen a ghost!'

89

'William, something's not right,' she replied. 'Look at the houses.'

William followed Brenda's gaze to all the familiar houses they passed every day and couldn't believe he hadn't noticed it sooner.

'Where are all the Christmas decorations?' Brenda asked.

There wasn't a single decoration hanging in any window, on any door, on any house on the street.

Holly wreaths had been tossed into flower beds. Fairy lights had been ripped from window frames, and there was only one snowman left standing. All the rest had been toppled to the ground.

'That fox must really *not* like Christmas decorations . . .' Brenda said.

'I'm starting to think it wasn't a fox after all,' William replied.

'If it wasn't a fox, then what was it?' Brenda asked.

'I don't know, but I've got a feeling it's something worse . . .' William said as the head of the last remaining snowman crashed to the pavement at their feet. 'Something a lot worse!'

CHAPTER TEN

DE-CHRISTMAS

William and Brenda arrived at school with tummies full of that nervous-rumbly feeling you get when you forget to eat breakfast. The fact they actually *had* forgotten to eat breakfast that morning only made their tummies *doubly nervous-rumbly*.

As they made their way to the school gates, they passed parents and grandparents who were busy nattering to each other. This wasn't unusual, of course, except instead of nattering about how little sleep they'd had that night or how bad the traffic was that morning, they were saying things like . . .

'We woke up and it was all gone!' one mum whispered.

'Not a single bauble left on our tree,' added a dad.

'Someone stole all the mini screwdriver sets out of our Christmas crackers. Now we've only got the fortune-telling fish left!' said another shocked grown-up, causing everyone around to gasp and shake their heads.

The school bell rang and, as he and Brenda headed inside for assembly, William spotted something comforting over the front door – a colourful banner made by Year Four that read:

SEASON'S GREETINGS TO EVERYBODY!
A HAPPY NEW YEAR TO ALL THE WORLD!

'Brenda, the school's Christmas decorations are still up!' William smiled as he pointed to the paper chains and tinsel dangling on the classroom doors they passed.

At the end of the hallway was the Project Table – a huge Christmas display of all the model villages and festive buildings the children had been working so hard on. Right in the centre was Brenda's masterpiece: her North Pole Snow Ranch!

'Good job too. If anyone touched my Christmas project, I'd . . .' Brenda made a fist. 'Well, I'd be straight back on that Naughty List.'

William made a mental note not to go anywhere near Brenda's model as they entered assembly, but his thoughts were interrupted by excited whispers fizzing around the room like electricity – because standing next to their headteacher, Miss Trustly, was a

POLICE OFFICER!

Everyone knows there are only two times that police officers show up at school:

1. *For planned visits where they talk about the police force and show you around the police car (and sometimes they even put a teacher in the back seat and pretend they're under arrest).*

OR

2. *When something serious has happened.*

There were no police visits planned.
This wasn't one of those educational talks.
This was not a drill.

'Good morning, students,' said Miss Trustly, who was looking a little nervous.

'*Good morning, miss,*' the children replied.

'By now you will all have noticed that we have a visitor, who has come to speak to you about . . .' Miss Trustly paused, searching for the right words. 'About something *strange*,' she said at last.

The entire hall gasped.

She tried again. 'I mean – something *worrying . . .*'

The children squeaked!

'Something . . . *mysterious!*' said Miss Trustly, unintentionally creating a frenzy in assembly with words that were already repeating in William's mind.

Strange . . .

Worrying . . .

Mysterious!

William had lots of experience with *strange*, *worrying* and *mysterious*. They had become like those unwelcome relatives that show up each Christmas, and William wasn't sure he was ready to spend another winter with them.

'Over to you, officer,' Miss Trustly said, stepping aside for the police officer to take centre stage.

'Hello, students. I am Sergeant Dwimble, and I'm here to talk to you about some of the . . . well, the *strange*, *worrying* and *mysterious* events that occurred last night.'

The assembly hall fell so silent you could have heard a bell jingle in the North Pole.

'Many of you woke up this morning to discover that your Christmas decorations had been vandalized. We want you to know that we have our best officers on the case, myself included.' Sergeant Dwimble beamed at them. 'And we are very confident that this will not happen again.'

BEEP! BEEP! BEEP! BEEP! BEEP! BEEP!

The school fire alarm suddenly blasted through the halls and, seconds later, the automatic sprinkler system burst into life, showering the entire school with freezing cold water.

There was screaming. There was running. There was

CHAOS!

'Stay calm!' Miss Trustly cried, as she wiped water from her glasses.

'Evacuate the building! Evacuate!' Sergeant Dwimble instructed, and William and Brenda followed the rest of the children out of the school hall, pushing past the caretaker, AKA Old Man Wrinkleface, who was grumblingly trudging through the wet corridors with his trusty mop. Soon they were all assembled in the playground, soggy but safe!

If having police at the school wasn't exciting enough, within minutes a huge fire engine arrived, lights on and siren blaring. The children cheered as the firefighters entered the school, but it wasn't long before they came back out.

'It appears to be a false alarm. No fire!' the chief firefighter announced, and everyone cheered again.

'Do we have a faulty sensor?' Miss Trustly asked.

'No, no. The sensors are all working fine,' the chief firefighter replied.

'If there was no fire and the sensors are working fine, then why did our alarm go off?' Miss Trustly frowned.

Suddenly a very soggy Old Man Wrinkleface stepped

out of the school with something in his hand, which he handed carefully to the chief firefighter. 'It appears that somebody set the alarm off on purpose, smashing the emergency button with *this*!'

The chief firefighter lifted the thing in the air for all the school to see. Something that made William's heart twitch.

'*Dad's litter-picker!*' William gasped, and Brenda elbowed him as if to say **SHHHHH!** as the chief firefighter showed the candy-cane-coloured litter-picker to Sergeant Dwimble, who placed it in a plastic bag marked *evidence*.

'Well, it's good news that there's no fire,' Miss Trustly said, putting on a brave smile.

'Yes, but I'm afraid the children are going to have to make some more Christmas decorations,' Old Man Wrinkleface said grimly. 'The sprinklers destroyed them completely.'

At that moment, the double doors to the school swung open and the rest of the firefighters emerged from the school, carrying the soggy remains of the Project Table.

William glanced at Brenda. She was frozen. Her hands had rolled up into tight fists as she watched what was left of her magical model snow ranch slop to the ground in glops of glittery gloop. The glue-icicles had come unstuck, the Christmasaurus's mane had washed away, and the crumpet walls in the tiny kitchen were the soggiest that any crumpets had ever been in the history of crumpets.

'Setting off the school sprinklers? Sounds like we've got a prankster,' Sergeant Dwimble said.

'Or someone who really doesn't like Christmas!' Miss Trustly replied, as Year Four's festive banner came unstuck and flapped unhappily to the ground.

'Maybe it was *Scrooge*,' the chief firefighter joked, making Sergeant Dwimble and Miss Trustly chuckle as he hunched over and pretended the litter-picker was his cane, just like Bob had done the night before when he'd brought Scrooge to life . . .

William had a thought.

One of those thoughts that seem to stop time.

'Well then, with all the classrooms being so wet, it looks like school is cancelled for the rest of today,' Miss

Trustly said, and the entire playground erupted into cheers once more.

Everyone except William and Brenda.

Brenda was still staring at her sloppy snow ranch remains, and William was still wondering.

'Brenda,' he whispered, tugging on her arm.

'William, can't you see I'm still sulking?' Brenda snapped dramatically.

'I need to talk to you,' he said urgently.

'Blimey, you look like you've seen a ghost,' she said, finally looking at his pale face.

A Christmasaurus Carol

William felt like he'd seen a ghost too. Three familiar ghosts – *Strange*, *Worrying* and *Mysterious*.

'Brenda, I have an idea who might be behind all this *de-Christmassing*, but you wouldn't believe it in a million years!' he said in a low voice.

'William, I've flown in Santa's sleigh pulled by a flying blue dinosaur. After that, I'll believe anything!' Brenda said, rolling her eyes.

'I think something bad might be happening.'

'Worse than broken decorations and soggy model snow ranches?'

'Way worse! I'll explain on the way,' William said, as he began to head across the playground.

'On the way where?'

'To prove the impossible,' William replied.

'Why does this feel like the start of another one of our Christmas adventures?' Brenda said with a twinkle of excitement in her eyes.

'Because I think it is,' William said, as he led Brenda away from school, back to the old, mysterious library.

CHAPTER ELEVEN

THE DISAPPEARING LIBRARY

William and Brenda were on a mission, navigating the busy streets packed with older children, who were heading home from their soggy school, and worried parents rushing to pick up the younger ones.

'I think there's something a little strange about that book,' William said.

'You mean the book you brought home last night?' Brenda asked.

'That's just it. I didn't bring that book home last night. *It brought itself home!*' William confessed.

'Are you saying you think it *walked* there? Or maybe *flew?*' Brenda asked, snorting, and William suddenly realized how ridiculous it sounded.

'I . . . I don't know what I think. All I know is I put that book back on the counter in the library, but somehow it managed to find its way to our house. Almost as though it wanted to be read!' he said.

'There's bound to be a simple explanation for all this. Now, show me this library of yours,' Brenda said,

rolling up her sleeves, ready to get down to business.

It was at times like this that William remembered just how much he liked having a sister. When there was a riddle to unravel, you could always rely on Brenda.

As they passed the hospital and turned on to the street that bordered Holly Heath on one side and Whiffington on the other, it was clear to William that, like every street in town, it didn't look like it had the night before. He began to play a real-life game of spot-the-difference in his mind, ticking off all the things that had changed.

Firstly, he noticed that Mr Ridley's reindeer decorations had decided to move from Whiffington to Holly Heath, as they were now sticking out of a hedge on the opposite side of the road to his house, instead of making a clatter on the roof.

Then he saw that Mrs Jones's dancing snowmen were dangling from the gutter.

He continued pointing out lots of other unmerry modifications to Brenda, but then he came to the most glaringly obvious difference of all.

'**THE LIBRARY!**' William gasped.

'Where?' asked Brenda.

'Exactly! It's . . . gone!' William said, looking into thin air.

'It can't have just vanished. You must have got the wrong street,' Brenda suggested.

'No, it was right here, between those two houses!' William pointed to where the library had stood the night before.

'*The night before!*' he blurted out.

'What?' Brenda asked.

'That's what it was called: *The Night-Before Library.*'

'The night before what?'

'I don't know. The night before . . . it *disappears*?' William suggested.

'The night before . . . all the Christmas decorations are trashed?' Brenda offered.

'The night before . . . a strange book follows you home,' William said.

They looked at each other for a moment before both saying: **'HOME!'**

They dashed back as fast as they could, weaving in and out of toppled Christmas trees and disgruntled people picking up the merry mess, and they didn't stop until they were inside the front door of their own wonky little house.

'What are you two doing home?' Bob said from the top of a ladder as he put the finishing touches on Christmas Tree Number Three. William could see that, as all their actual decorations had been crunched and smashed into thousands of glittering pieces, Bob had taken matters into his own hands and had spent the morning creating hundreds of amazing homemade paper decorations.

'Why aren't you at school?' Pamela asked, as William and Brenda caught their breath in the doorway.

'It . . . got . . . cancelled,' Brenda gasped.

'Why? Has something happened?' Bob said, stepping down from the ladder, looking concerned.

'No . . . time . . . to . . . explain. Where is it?' asked William.

'Where's what?' Bob replied.

'The library book from last night. *A Christmas Carol*!' William said frantically.

'It's still in your room, where I left it,' Bob said, but William and Brenda were already halfway down the hall and in William's bedroom before Bob and Pamela had caught up with them.

'There it is,' William said, spotting the book lying open in the middle of his bedroom floor.

'That's strange,' Bob said. 'I don't remember leaving it open.'

'No, just like I didn't remember bringing it home,' William added.

'William, are you trying to say that you think this book is . . . *alive*?' Brenda asked.

'No, don't be ridiculous!' William replied, and everyone breathed a sigh of relief. 'I think some-one *inside* the book is alive.'

There was silence.

William felt Bob, Pamela and Brenda all staring at him. Then, when they saw that he was being serious, their eyes returned to the book.

But William had spotted something else.

'Or, at least, someone who *was* inside the book . . .' he said, with a slight nervous tremble in his voice as he pointed at the floor.

'Are those . . . *footprints*?' Bob gasped.

They all leant in closer to inspect the marks that were now clearly visible on the wooden floor of William's room.

They were indeed footprints.

And, as clear as snow, the first one began at the edge of the open book, leading away and out of the bedroom door.

'Who on earth do they belong to?' Pamela whispered, clearly feeling the same chill run down her back as William felt.

'I don't know, but I'm calling Sergeant Dwimble. We're not having strangers wandering around our house,' Bob said firmly.

'Dad, I don't think this was a stranger. I think this is someone that you know very well,' William said, taking a breath to steady himself.

'Who?' Bob replied.

Brenda shifted her gaze from the footprints to William – and began to nod. 'You told us all about him last night, Bob,' she said, starting to understand William's theory.

'I know it sounds completely nutcrackers, Dad, but there's only one person who hates Christmas enough to pull down a family's Christmas decorations in the night.'

'Or to soak a model Christmas village!' Brenda grumbled.

They all glanced down again, following the footprints back to the open pages of the book, as if someone had stepped out of it.

'You don't mean . . .' Bob said, and William watched as his dad finally realized who this person was – the person that you've probably guessed already. 'Ebenezer Scrooge?'

William and Brenda nodded together.

'B-b-but that's impossible!' Bob stuttered nervously. 'I don't believe it. I *won't* believe it! I need proof. Hard evidence!'

'Like this?' Pamela said, as she picked up something in the corner of William's bedroom and turned to show it to the family.

It was a long, wooden walking cane, with a simple curved, worn metal handle. About halfway down, the cane had splintered and was snapped in half.

'No . . . it can't be!' Bob squeaked.

'Oh yes it can! Look at the initials engraved in the

handle,' Pamela said, holding up the top half of the cane so that everyone could read the two clear letters –

E. S.

'*Ebenezer Scrooge!*' everyone said together.

'It's broken. That explains why the other cane was at school!' Brenda said.

'What *other cane?*' asked Bob.

'Your one – the litter-picker! It was found at our school. I bet old Scroogey scampered out of the book *here* –' Brenda started to re-enact the events like she was solving a crime – 'then he stumbled here. Look at the footprints!'

Brenda pointed at the footprints that clearly ran into the edge of William's wardrobe. 'He fell, snapping his cane in half, saw your litter-picker, swapped it – and he was off!' she said, a big, satisfied grin on her face for having worked out the riddle.

The Disappearing Library

'So, it's true . . . Scrooge is on the loose, and *it's all my fault!*' Bob whimpered, before fainting face-first on to William's bedroom floor.

Chapter Twelve
SCROOGE-VISION

It wasn't long before the winter sun was setting. William had spent most of the day nursing his understandably fainty father back to consciousness. The problem was that poor Bob would take one look at the footprints around the open book and go all wobbly-kneed and flimsy-headed again – and – **BOFF!** There he'd go. Another one bites the bauble!

So, let's leave the Trundles for a moment while they help Bob, and head past the streets filled with Christmas devastation to the other end of Holly Heath, where Christmas trees still stood proudly and tinsel still glinted merrily . . . for the time being, at least. A familiar sound was drawing nearer, *click-clacking* through the streets.

CLICK-CLACK!

That's right. We heard them at the very beginning of this story: Scrooge's footsteps! Except they weren't *click-clacking* on old London cobbles inside a book any more. Those footsteps were out in the real world now, and it was a far more Christmassy world than the one these old footsteps were used to *click-clacking* through.

There were twinkly lights in every window, merry music was drifting from every shop, and sweet smells were in the air, not to mention pictures of Santa with his jolly smile on every bus-stop billboard in town.

To your eyes, this stuff probably looks fantastically festive. It's the stuff that makes us feel that excited Christmassy feeling each year. But if you were looking through Scrooge's cold, narrow eyes, you would have seen it very differently. Here, try these special Scrooge-goggles on for a moment, and let's take a look at the town through *Scrooge-Vision* . . .

Ergh! *Those lights are repulsive, flashing in those utterly disgusting colours – revolting reds and grotesque greens. Why does everything need to be colourful at this ridiculous time of year? What's wrong with grey?!*

And what are those sickeningly sweet smells? It's enough to put a person off their bowl of gruel.

*All this . . . this . . . **stuff** is just a waste of time. And, even worse, it's a waste of money!*

Christmas has become nothing more than an infestation of manufactured merriness, poisoning these houses and the weak minds of all the fools who occupy them. It is time-stealing, money-wasting, irresponsible twaddle, and the world would be better off without some old fool falling down chimneys once a year with a sack full of toys and chocolates that will only rot children's teeth and their already-rotted brains.

*And now what's that racket I hear . . . **Christmas carols?** Of all the pointless things I loathe about Christmas, music is possibly the thing I detest most of all! Rhymes are for nursery rhymes, and nursery rhymes are for babies – and therefore so is Christmas. It's for babies who will grow up to be even bigger babies. If nursery rhymes are what they want, then how about this one?*

'Humbug here, humbug there.

Humbug, humbug everywhere . . .'

Take them off!

TAKE THEM OFF!

TAKE THEM OFF!

Are you back? Has the Scrooge-Vision worn off?

Phew!

How do you feel? Scroogey? Well, I'm not surprised. It only takes a few minutes of Scrooge-Vision to make you angry at the world. I think that's enough Scrooge-Vision for one day, don't you?

But what if you couldn't turn Scrooge-Vision off? What if that was just the way you looked at the world all day, every day? Well, that's what made Ebenezer Scrooge the way he was, because, for him, Scrooge-Vision was just . . . vision!

As those footsteps *click-clacked* through the streets of the real world, they were accompanied by a shadow: a miserably hunched shadow that swiftly moved past the merrily decorated houses.

'*Humbug*,' Scrooge growled, as he whipped a beautifully decorated wreath from a front door and threw it like a Frisbee into the wheelie bin, before marching towards the next house.

'Oi! That's my Christmas reef!' barked a man who had appeared in the now-wreathless doorway.

His real name was Bruce Nutbog, but his friends called him *Bruise*. Why? Because if someone upset him, they would get – you guessed it – a **BRUISE**!

As mean as Bruise looked, though, he had a soft spot for one thing: Christmas. So throwing Bruise's Christmas wreath in the bin was definitely one sure way to get him to live up to his name!

'What's the matter, darlin'?' called his wife from inside their house.

'Nuffin', love. Just someone lookin' for trouble,' Bruise said, as he marched down his front steps and pulled his now-not-so-pretty wreath out of the bin.

'My reef!' Bruise gasped at the straggly holly leaves and twigs that poked out in all directions. 'My bootiful Christmas reef! It was so merry an' jolly an' twinkly, but now it's . . . ruined.'

Bruise was angry. His face looked like a thermometer left in the hot sun, turning redder and redder as he bounded towards Scrooge, cracking his knuckles, which had letters tattooed on each one – **NORTY** and **NICE** – and which were ready to biff the grouchy old humbug on his nose . . .

. . . but as Bruise neared this shadowy wreath thief, he heard a whisper in the wintry night – a single word that chilled him to his very core.

'Hhhhummmmbuuuuuug . . .'

Scrooge breathed the icy word through the air like a spell, and it settled on Bruise's ears like a winter frost and spread to his brain, freezing his love of Christmas.

Bruise stumbled back like he'd received one of his own nose-biffs, except the bruise this one left was on the inside.

'What on earf is this rubbish?' Bruise growled as he inspected his own Christmas wreath again. 'Shiny? *Ergh!* Twinkly? *Repulsive!* Merry? **BAH HUMBUG!**' Bruise sounded exactly like Scrooge himself, as though somehow Scrooge's own miserableness had floated through the air and seeped into him. It was as though Bruise was suddenly seeing his precious wreath through **Scrooge-Vision!**

Bruise scrunched up the wreath in his tattooed fists, which had changed too, and now read **NORTY** and **NORTY**.

If that weren't bad enough, as the '*HUMBUG*' hissed through Bruise's lips, it seemed to send a shockwave of Scroogeness across the street, causing all surrounding fairy lights to flicker and fade, nearby Christmas trees to wilt, and baubles to swell and burst like over-inflated balloons!

Under the dark shadow cast by the brim of Scrooge's top hat, the flickering fairy lights flashed upon a glimpse of a grin. A gross, grim, greedy grin that revelled in watching this unhappiness spread – as if this were only just the start of something wildly wicked.

CHAPTER THIRTEEN

A WILDLY
WICKED WEEK

William woke up with a headache after a long night of watching his dad pace around the house, trying to figure out what to do.

'It's impossible!' Bob would suddenly laugh to himself, flinging his arms in the air as though the idea that Scrooge might *actually* have been pulled into existence was nothing more than an irritating fly buzzing around the room that he could just swat away.

Seconds later, his laughter would turn to despair. 'But the footprints! The book! The C-C-C-Christmas tree!'

He would then break down at the base of Christmas Tree Number . . . OK, I've totally lost count of the back-up trees, but the point is that Bob was having a very hard time coming to terms with the fact that the person who was famous for detesting Christmas more than anyone might be lurking right around the corner.

And William knew exactly why his dad was feeling so rotten about it.

'Dad, it's not your fault,' William said to Bob for the seventeenth time that morning, as they all sat glumly around the breakfast table.

'But *I* was the one who read that *thing*!' Bob said, pointing his finger at the mysterious green book in the centre of the table, where it now seemed to glow ever so slightly. 'If that's where Scrooge came from, then I must have been the one to let him out!'

William's brain was wandering back to the night the library had appeared, and the words he'd said just before he'd spotted it for the first time were bouncing around his head . . .

'*I wish Christmas would just* **GO AWAY**!'

Bob might have read the book, but William couldn't

help but think that his wish might have somehow summoned it. Before he could confess, though, Pamela spotted something on the TV.

BREAKING NEWS flashed up in big, bold letters as a news reporter appeared with a very concerned frown.

'We interrupt the scheduled programme to bring you the worrying news that there have been reports of a disturbance across London,' announced news reporter Stan Walker.

'Across *London*?' Bob gasped. 'No, surely Scrooge hasn't already reached *London*?'

'Decorations have been disappearing from homes, displays have been stolen from shop windows and the Oxford Street Christmas lights are . . . gone!' the news reporter said.

'Gone?' Pamela gasped.

'Not the Oxford Street lights. Those are my favourite!' Bob whimpered.

'We're going live now to Oxford Street where our reporter Kelly McGowan is speaking to witnesses,' Stan Walker continued. 'Kelly, what's the latest on the ground?'

'Thank you, Stan. It's a grey morning here in London, made even greyer by the lack of Christmas displays that were illuminating these shop windows until they vanished in the early hours of the morning. I'm here with Alonso, a shop owner. Alonso, can you tell me how it feels to have been the victim of such a miserable anti-Christmas crime?'

'Well, I think whoever did this to Oxford Street . . . has done us all a favour!' Alonso said with a thin smile.

Kelly, the reporter, looked about as stunned as William felt.

'I'm sorry. Did you say the Christmas thief has done us all a *favour*?' Kelly asked, making sure she'd heard Alonso correctly.

'Yeah! This is my shop right here,' Alonso said, pointing to his now-empty shop window. 'It's usually covered in twenty-thousand fairy lights all twinklin' and sparklin' twenty-four seven!'

'Sounds lovely.'

'I used to think that too, until this morning when I realized it's all a bit bright and garish. Plus, it takes a whole bloomin' day to put 'em up at the start of

December, then, before you know it, we're taking 'em down again. What's the point?' Alonso said.

'Isn't *Christmas* the point?' Kelly suggested.

'*Christmas? Bah humbug!*'

And, as those words left Alonso's lips, Kelly staggered back a little, like she'd lost her balance.

'Kelly, are you OK? Has something happened?' Stan Walker asked from the safety of the newsroom.

'Yes . . . yes! I'm fine. It's just that . . . suddenly I understand Alonso's frustration. Christmas must be such an annoyance for you. For all of London!' Kelly said, and Alonso nodded. 'So, you're actually feeling relieved to wake up to find one of London's most Christmassy streets totally clear of Christmas?'

'Of course! Now we can just carry on like Christmas never happens!' Alonso said.

'Well, there you have it. This is Kelly McGowan, reporting live from Oxford Street, where it seems that the Christmas spirit is well and truly gone, and the locals are happy to see the back of it! Over to you in the studio!' Kelly said, finishing her report.

The Trundles stared at one another in horror.

'Did you see that?' William cried. 'When that shop owner said *"Bah humbug!"* it was like it hypnotized the reporter!'

'Taking away her Christmas spirit,' agreed Brenda.

'This is bad,' Pamela said, looking at Bob.

'Really bad!' William added.

But what William didn't know yet was that Oxford Street was just the tip of the snowflake, and that this was the start of a wildly wicked week for Scrooge.

Each morning when the Trundles sat down for breakfast, there was yet another 'breaking news' announcement revealing the latest unmerry events:

Sunday: BREAKING NEWS – The annual Christmas jumper competition in Knitsville has been cancelled due to the unravelling of every woolly sweater in town. Locals say it'll be a total itch-fest trying to wind it all up.

Monday: BREAKING NEWS – A Christmas lights switch-on has been called off due to ten-thousand light bulbs being stolen. Organizers tried to come up with an alternative plan, but no one had any bright ideas.

A WILDLY WICKED WEEK

❋ *Tuesday: BREAKING NEWS – The ice-skating rink outside the Natural History Museum has melted. People skating at the time were in floods of tears and an eyewitness said, 'It was not cool.'*

❋ *Wednesday: BREAKING NEWS – All the sausages were stolen from a German Christmas market overnight. Event organizers said it was their wurst nightmare.*

❋ *Thursday: BREAKING NEWS – Due to poor ticket sales, Christmas pantomimes across the UK have been suspended . . . Oh yes they have!*

Despite William and Brenda's best efforts, they hadn't managed to find Scrooge. With each breaking news story Bob would cry '*To the Trundle-mobile!*', which was what he called their old banger of a car that only just had enough room for them all to squeeze inside. Nevertheless, they'd cram in and zoom from town to town, city to city, following what William had called *Scrooge's Trail of Humbug*. They travelled everywhere from Holly Heath to Greyville . . . even to a strange place called Freaky over on the dangerous side of town! But Scrooge was always one step ahead.

By Friday, the whole country was starting to feel so un-Christmassy it almost felt like **JANUARY** – and everyone knows that January is rubbish!

'Please, no more!' William said, as the Trundles gathered for breakfast on the morning of Christmas Eve, and Bob switched on the news to see the words **BREAKING NEWS** on the screen.

'This just in,' announced Stan Walker. 'For anyone who's still interested in Christmas, we're getting reports of more unusual unfestive activity that happened last night. Our correspondent, Kelly McGowan, has all the latest on the situation unfolding in Whiffington Town.'

'Whiffington? But that's the next town – only a few streets away!' Brenda gasped.

'So that means . . .' William started to think. 'Scrooge must be heading back this way!'

CHAPTER FOURTEEN
A WHISPER IN WHIFFINGTON

Some towns and cities are famous for different reasons. Stonehaven near Aberdeen is famous for the world's first deep-fried Mars bar. Liverpool is famous for its music scene. Whiffington is famous for rubbish!

That's right: *rubbish*. The stuff you chuck. The debris you dump. The litter you scatter. The trash you toss. The . . . you get the idea.

Whiffington is famous for rubbish because underneath the clouds of green pong from glorious recyclable refuse, at the very centre of Whiffington, is the town's beating heart – the dump! And it was there, at Whiffington Dump, that news correspondent Kelly McGowan and her team were reporting live on the worrying events that were seemingly spreading across the country – and there was clear evidence of it in the rubbish.

'The Whiffington Waste Management Company are claiming there has been an alarming spike in the amount of Christmas trees being dumped at their site today,' Kelly McGowan reported from beside a big green rubbish truck that was overflowing with Christmas trees, most of them still fully decorated.

'I'm here with the owner of Whiffington Waste Management, Larry Dungston. Can you tell me exactly what's been happening here in Whiffington?' asked Kelly, pointing her microphone at Mr Dungston's gloriously grubby face.

'Well, it was my daughter, Lucy, who noticed it first. She comes on the rubbish-collection rounds with me, you see,' Mr Dungston said, nudging his daughter to speak up.

A WHISPER IN WHIFFINGTON

William thought that Lucy Dungston looked to be about the same age as himself and Brenda, with an adventurous spark in her eye that he liked very much.

'Usually, we pick up bags of the same old rubbish – mouldy bread crusts, empty milk cartons, scraps from yesterday's dinners,' Lucy explained. 'But this morning as we drove around town I saw wheelie bin after wheelie bin overflowing with *Christmas* stuff.'

'I see. But isn't it normal for people to have more rubbish around Christmas?' Kelly McGowan asked.

'Oh, sure, but this wasn't rubbish. People were throwing away *nice* things, *new* things, *Christmassy* things, before Christmas is even over!' Lucy cried. 'Just take a look at this . . .' She walked to the back of the big green truck and started pulling out some of the things the people of Whiffington had chucked.

'From one street alone we picked up twenty-two snow globes, seventeen flying-angel ornaments, nine fairy-light garlands, over forty stockings –'

'And a partridge in a pear tree!' added Mr Dungston.

'Do you know the reason behind this sudden desire to dump Christmas?' Kelly asked.

'Not a clue!' said Mr Dungston. 'Us Whiffingtonians love Christmas! Well, we used to – but after last night no one has any decorations left. Not a tree in sight. They're all at our dump!'

'There have been reports from some Whiffington residents of a strange noise during the night, a sort of whisper in the air. Is this something either of you witnessed?' Kelly asked.

William saw Lucy and her dad exchange a look, as though they knew something but were too nervous to say it out loud.

A Whisper in Whiffington

'You *did* hear the whisper?' Kelly said, pushing her microphone towards Mr Dungston.

'Well, noises in the night aren't unusual around here. Whiffington is a creaky old town. But Lucy and I are up before anyone else and, well, we did hear *something* . . . but it could have just been the wind.'

'It was a *whisper*, Dad!' Lucy insisted.

'I see! And who was it that was whispering?' Kelly McGowan asked, aiming the mic at Lucy.

'That's the thing. There wasn't anybody else around,' Lucy said. 'It was as though the air itself was whispering, like a voice travelling by shadows and fog.'

'What was it saying?' Kelly McGowan enquired.

'Well, once I started my engine we couldn't make it out. We had work to do, and rubbish trucks are noisy beasts!' Mr Dungston said, banging his green truck with pride.

'Whatever it was saying, though, seems to have made people around here want to forget the meaning of Christmas!' Lucy said, leaning into her dad's grubby high-vis jacket for comfort.

'What do you mean, Lucy?' asked the reporter, nudging the mic closer.

'Well, Christmas isn't something you can just throw away. It's not a tree or a glittery decoration. It's more of a *feeling*. Whatever you believe, Christmas is a moment we share each year, when we all agree to forget our differences and be kind to each other. If people want to throw *that* away, then we're *all* in the dumps!' Lucy said.

'Then what would you say to people out there on this Un-Christmas Eve who haven't forgotten the meaning of Christmas . . . yet?' the reporter asked.

Lucy cleared her throat and looked straight down the camera, almost as though she were speaking directly to William, who was watching from his kitchen, in the next town over.

'If you're watching this and you still love Christmas, if you still want to pull crackers tomorrow, eat too much chocolate, sing Christmas carols and get presents from Santa, then we're going to need help before it's too . . .'

Lucy stopped speaking. Her head tilted like she'd just heard something.

'*Hhhhhhuuuuummmmmmm . . .*'

'I heard it too, Lucy. The *whisper*!' said Mr Dungston.

'*. . . buuuuuuuuuuuuuuuug!*'

A Whisper in Whiffington

'People watching at home,' announced Kelly McGowan, 'a strange fog has just blown in and it's accompanied by the strangest sound . . . I can confirm that it does indeed sound like a whisper, but it's hard to make out what it's saying . . .'

She listened closely as the wind suddenly howled and a strong gust caused the cameraman to lose his footing. The camera fell to the ground. On TV at home, all that could be seen were the feet of Lucy and Mr Dungston scrambling into their rubbish truck for safety, as a whispering voice on the wind crackled half a word –

'*Hhhhhhhummmmmbuuuuu–*'

And with that, the breaking-news report from Whiffington went off-air.

Chapter Fifteen
ASH

William still had Lucy's words ringing in his ears as he looked at the creepy copy of *A Christmas Carol* on the kitchen table, its subtle green glow casting an eerie light on everyone's faces.

'All those poor Christmas trees, just dumped!' Bob said, quickly leaving the room with a tear in his eye.

William knew he had to do something.

'That kid, Lucy, is right. We're going to need help!' he said, nodding like a decision had been made.

Pamela shook her head. 'Who could possibly help with this?'

'When Christmas needs saving, there's only one person

you can trust. Well, one person and a dinosaur,' said William, and with that he pulled out a pen and paper and started writing an urgent letter to the North Pole.

Dear Santa,

It's me, William. Sorry to write again but . . . well, there's no easy way to say this, so here it goes. Brace yourself . . .

We accidentally released Ebenezer Scrooge from an old copy of A Christmas Carol and now he's on the loose, sucking the joy out of Christmas.

I know it's Christmas Eve, but if we don't stop him TONIGHT then there's a good chance that we'll all wake up tomorrow and NOT CARE ABOUT CHRISTMAS ANY MORE!

We need your help. Please, come as fast as you can (Chrissy too, of course).

We need to save Christmas . . . again!

WILLIAM TRUNDLE

Ash

William sealed the letter in an envelope and wrote

'Santa's Snow Ranch, North Pole, URGENT'

in big letters on the front.

'Wait a minute! It's Christmas Eve! This letter will never get to the North Pole in time!' he suddenly realized.

'This is urgent. You need to send this via the emergency Christmas post!' Bob said, coming back into the kitchen, wiping his eyes with a hanky.

William and Brenda blinked at Bob as though he'd lost his sprouts.

'The *what*?' William asked.

'You didn't think the only way to reach Santa was to put your letter in the postbox, did you? My goodness, have I not taught you anything about Christmas?' Bob said, shaking his head. 'Follow me and bring that letter!'

Bob grabbed a box of matches from the kitchen drawer and dashed into the living room, where he made them all gather around the fireplace.

'We're not going up the chimney, are we?' Pamela asked.

'*We're* not, but that letter is!' Bob explained. 'When you need to ask Santa for help, you need *this* . . .'

He reached underneath the pile of logs in the unlit fireplace and scooped up a handful of black ash.

'Ash? What do we need ash for?' Brenda scoffed.

'You need ash because you want to ask Santa for help . . .' Bob smiled as he used the charred chips of charcoal to write some words on the fireplace tiles.

Ask Santa for Help

'ASH!' William whispered with wonder.

'Just when I thought I knew absolutely everything about Christmas, you go and blow my merry mind!' Brenda said.

'What do we do with it?' William asked, tightly clutching his very important letter. 'This needs to get to Santa **ASAP**!'

'I'll show you, but move back!' Bob said, waiting for William and Brenda to follow his instructions before striking a match and throwing it into the pile of logs, starting a small fire in the hearth. 'Now, before I tell you what comes next, you must promise me *never to start a fire yourself. And never to get too close to a fire, or to mess around with fire in any way –*'

'We promise, Dad!' William said, already knowing full well not to play with fire.

'Even in a Christmas emergency!' Bob added, looking very serious.

'Dad! We promise!' William said, flapping his letter at Bob.

'All right – put it in!' Bob said, nodding at the letter in William's hands.

William frowned. 'In the fire?'

'Now you're just making this up!' Brenda huffed.

'I'm not! It's the truth,' Bob said. 'The fastest way to get a letter to Santa is to put it in the fire and send it up the chimney! How do you think children used to write to Santa before the Royal Mail was invented?'

William looked at his letter, then at the flickering flames of the fire.

'All right, as long as you're sure it won't just burn up into nothing!' he said doubtfully.

'That's exactly what you *want* it to do! The flames will burn it up into teeny, tiny particles, then *swoosh*! Up the chimney it goes, into the sky, across the world, a million times the speed of post until it reaches Santa's own chimney,' Bob told him.

'Then what happens?'

'Well, no one really knows. We'd have to ask Santa to be sure, but I've no doubt it involves some sort of mysterious magic that unjumbles all the burnt pieces of ash and reverses the process until they turn back into a letter for Santa to read.'

William positioned himself in front of the warm fire and took a breath.

'OK, here it goes. Santa, we need your help!' William said, and with that he gently threw his emergency letter into the fire and watched as the paper became food for the flames before turning black, breaking into tiny pieces, then floating up the chimney and out into the sky, where it caught a southerly wind and was carried north . . .

Chapter Sixteen

FIRE

Way up north, just seconds after William had popped his letter into the fire, shiny black specks started to flicker beneath the stockings over the fireplace of Santa's living room.

'What the Dickens?' Santa cried with surprise, leaping from his seat and spilling a jug-sized mug of hot chocolate over his red onesie.

'Oooh, I wonder who is using ASH!' he said, ringing out his chocolatey beard as he twirled eagerly towards the sparks in the hearth.

The Christmasaurus padded into the room, sniffing the sooty air as though he'd picked up a familiar scent.

He gave Santa a worried look. Ever since the line in the sky had appeared in the North Pole, danger had felt on the horizon and now there was an urgent ASH letter? 'I'm sure it'll just be someone adding a last-minute present to their Christmas list.' Santa said, trying to reassure his dino friend. 'I used to get all my post this way, but not many people remember the *Ask Santa for Help* process these days. It's an old system, but *look*! It still works as well as the day we installed it!' As he spoke, more silvery-black flakes of shimmering ash floated magically down the chimney like snow and landed neatly in the hearth.

'Ho, ho, ho! We'd better call the **FIRE** service!'

Santa clapped his hands together. 'Chrissy, give that bell a jingle!'

Santa pointed to a little golden bell that was attached to the side of the fireplace with the letters **FIRE** embossed on its surface.

The Christmasaurus swung his tail and rung the bell.

DING-A-LING-A-LING!

There was a rumbling in the distance, then the sound of sirens approaching.

'Here they come! Here they come!' Santa grinned as the door burst open and an elf-sized fire engine screeched into the living room!

The worry the Christmasaurus had felt a moment ago was forgotten, as the engine's lights flashed pine green and candy-cane red. Through the windows, Santa and the Christmasaurus could see the team of highly trained, very serious-looking **FIRE** service elves.

'You're in for a real treat, Chrissy. These elves don't get out much!' Santa whispered, as the fire engine skidded to a halt at the edge of the fireplace and, one by one, six elves leapt out of the engine and started to sing:

A Christmasaurus Carol

'If something's happened, something bad,
First run and tell your mum or dad
Or any grown-up that you know,
Then you need to shout like so:

F. I. R. E.

Festive Instant Response Emergency!

Maybe someone burnt the turkey
Or sprouts have made your bottom burpy.
When Christmas turns into disaster,
Who'll make it Merrily Ever After?

F. **I.** **R.** **E.**

Festive Instant Response Emergency!

Perhaps your stocking has a hole
Or your snowman lost his coal.
We've fixed worse and seen it all.
The only team you need to call:

F. **I.** **R.** **E.**

Festive Instant Response Emergency!'

The song went on for another ten minutes while the
FIRE service elves unloaded their equipment from

their engine. Ladders were placed around the fireplace, a long length of red hose was unravelled, and
the team ended the song by falling into line at Santa's
slippers.

'Bravo-ho-ho!' Santa clapped, wiping a tear from his
eye. He loved a song and dance.

> **'Santa Claus, Your Merriness,**
> **We're here to sort this festive mess!'**

said Sootfoot, the chief FIRE service inspector, with
a salute.

'At ease, Sootfoot. It appears we have been sent a letter
via ASH that will need unburning and recombobulating,'
Santa said, pointing to the black flakes.

> **'If something's cindered, we'll undo it.**
> **Prepare the hose with emalf fluid!'**

Sootfoot sang, and his team started climbing the
ladders next to the fireplace and passing up the
long reel of red hose. It was connected to a large

tank on the back of the engine with the words **Emalf Fluid – Highly Unflammable** printed on the side.

The Christmasaurus hid behind Santa's ginormous bottom as the elves got ready to switch on the hose.

'Oh, don't be scared, Chrissy. Emalf fluid simply reverses the effects of flames. It's essential in my line of work. Wouldn't set foot near a chimney without it!' Santa said, as Sootfoot gave the signal and the elves began pumping the flame-reversing potion on to the charred remains of William's letter.

'Look! Look, Chrissy! It's working! Ho, ho!' Santa cheered, as the magical emalf fluid coated the ashes, washing away the black flakes, reversing them until they started revealing the white paper it used to be.

'This is my favourite part!' Santa said, rubbing his hands in excitement as the pieces of paper pulled closer together as though they were magnetically attracted to each other. Piece by piece, the paper uncreased itself, returning perfectly to its original state before floating up into the air, folding itself in half and sliding into its envelope.

'That'll do! Thank you, **FIRE** service, you've been most helpful. Go and help yourselves to some fresh crumpets in the kitchen,' Santa said, and Sootfoot gave him another salute while his team rolled up the hose and packed away the ladders before zooming off to the kitchen.

'Now then, let's see who could be in need of some help,' Santa said, opening his letter. 'Ah, it's our good friend William! Oh dear . . .'

The Christmasaurus's icy mane perked up. Was William in trouble?

'This doesn't sound good. Not good at all. In fact, it sounds absolutely disasterrific . . . You were right to be worried, Chrissy – this must be the trouble we sensed in the stars!'

Santa leapt to the window and peered between the curtains at the sky. The dark line that had appeared through the Northern Lights had grown even bigger. 'Jingle my bells, why didn't I do something sooner?! Starlump! Specklehump!' Santa boomed, and the two elves appeared instantly, as though they'd been there the whole time.

FIRE

'What took you so long?! The Christmasaurus and I are leaving,' Santa announced, and Starlump immediately fainted into Specklehump's arms.

> 'Santa! Santa! You can't leave!
> There's no time – it's Christmas Eve!'

Specklehump said, while trying to bring Starlump around.

'I know, and that's precisely why we *must* leave straight away, for if we don't, then we might be delivering presents to people who won't care about Christmas any more!' Santa explained.

> 'B-b-but how can you fly away?
> We've just begun to load the sleigh!'

groaned Starlump, who had finally come round.

> 'What can we do to fix this mess?
> We need to send an SOS!'

Specklehump added.

153

'An SOS? Jolly jingle bells, you're right, Specklehump!'

Santa reached up and tugged on one of the stockings hanging in the fireplace.

Suddenly there was a **CRACK** and a **HISS** and the entire fireplace revolved, taking Santa, the Christmasaurus and the two elves into a **VERY TOP-SECRET** room.

CHAPTER SEVENTEEN
SANTA'S OTHER SLEIGH

All right, before we carry on you need to know that what I'm about to tell you is so top secret that it could get me in a lot of trouble for writing it in this book – not even Santa's elves know about it. So, I'm only going to continue the rest of this chapter if you promise you won't tell anyone . . . not a jingle?

A Christmasaurus Carol

Then repeat after me:

I, _____, hereby promise not to tell a living person, elf, reindeer, fairy, dinosaur or any other magical creature about the top-secret information that I am about to read.

Cross my heart and hope to get no Christmas presents!

OK – thanks for your cooperation. Let's continue . . .

Santa flicked a switch and a million multicoloured lights flickered to life, illuminating this **VERY TOP-SECRET** room.

The Christmasaurus, Specklehump and Starlump couldn't believe their eyes as they stepped into this unknown part of Santa's Snow Ranch.

'Welcome to my secret holiday hideout, my fortress of festiveness: *Santa's Sanctorum!*' Santa cheered.

The Christmasaurus let out a little huff.

'Oh, don't be cross with me! *Nobody* knows about this place, Chrissy. It's only for super-duper Christmas emergencies, and that's exactly what today is!' Santa said. 'In here, we'll find anything and everything we could possibly need!'

'But Santa, do you mean to say
Somewhere in here is . . .'

'Another sleigh!' Santa finished Starlump's rhyme as he pulled back a huge dust sheet to reveal a slick, sleek, sparkling sleigh.

'Ta-da! Isn't she marvellous? Isn't she splenderrific? Isn't she sleigh-tastic?' Santa gushed as he skipped around this secret sleigh.

The Christmasaurus sniffed the glossy green paintwork. There was no compartment for toys, and only one seat, which resembled the cockpit of a jet plane. It even had two small jet engines at the back for added lift, and along the side were three large letters: **SOS**.

'This is SOS – *Santa's Other Sleigh!*' Santa beamed.

'It's not like trusty old Red, no, no. This one isn't designed to deliver presents and doesn't need a whole team of reindeer to pull it.'

The Christmasaurus growled.

'Ho, ho, it's all right! This sleigh still needs to be pulled along, and I think one very strong, very special dinosaur should just about manage.' Santa winked, and the Christmasaurus's mood quickly changed to excitement as he circled this new secret flying machine. 'Right then, Starlump, Specklehump, hitch up Chrissy to the SOS.'

Santa's loyal elves leapt to work getting the sleigh flight-ready, while Santa tugged another stocking

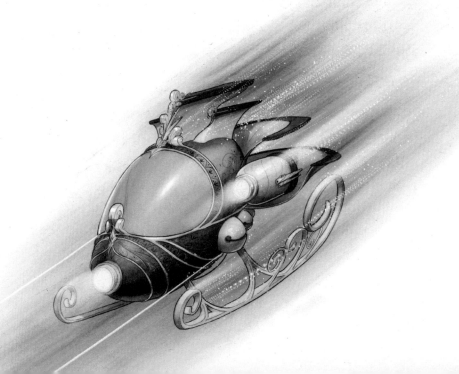

hanging on the fireplace. The bricks in the chimney magically *clinked* and *clonked* as they opened up to reveal a take-off path to the starry sky.

'While we're gone, don't stop preparing the other sleigh,' he told the two elves. 'Load the presents, strap up the reindeer, and we'll be back in time for Christmas Eve deliveries! We'll just nip down to young William, find that pesky Scrooge, pop him back in his book and be home before you can say *humbug*, with plenty of time to deliver those presents!' Santa said confidently.

The Christmasaurus gave a little roar of joy as he slipped into the harness and readied himself to fly.

Santa climbed into the cockpit of the SOS, turned on the radio and tuned into his favourite station – Christmas FM, which played non-stop Christmas hits. The moment the magical, merry music filled the room, the sleigh lifted off the floor as though it were desperate to get going.

**'The weather is clear in the North Pole sky.
The sleigh is set and ready to fly!'**

sang Starlump and Specklehump.

159

A Christmasaurus Carol

'Right then, Christmasaurus, let's go-HO-HO!' Santa bellowed at the top of his voice, and the Christmasaurus launched into the air, effortlessly pulling Santa's Other Sleigh behind him.

They circled the secret room before zooming up the open chimney and out into the sky. The Christmasaurus turned this way, then that, getting a feel for this new, smaller, sleeker, *speedier* sleigh.

'All right, Chrissy, let's see what this thing can –'

Santa didn't have to finish his sentence as the Christmasaurus launched forward at the speed of Northern Lights, heading for his best friend, William.

CHAPTER EIGHTEEN

AN UNINVITED GUEST

William, Brenda, Bob and Pamela were still sitting by the fireplace in their living room after watching the ashes of William's letter flitter away up the chimney, when there was a clatter on the roof.

'Did you hear that?' William said.

Brenda nodded.

Thud! Thud!

'There it is again!' Bob whispered. 'It sounded like it came from the –'

CRASH!

A Christmasaurus Carol

Suddenly a cloud of soot puffed down the chimney, filling the fireplace with a black fog. Within it, William saw two big, blue eyes blinking out at him.

'Christmasaurus!' William cheered as his dinosaur friend leapt towards him with such force that he almost knocked William out of his chair!

'Wow, you got here fast!' Brenda said as an enormous sooty Santa squeezed out of the fireplace.

'You came!' William smiled. 'I wasn't sure if you would. I mean, it's Christmas Eve, after all.'

'My dear William, Christmas is the time of year you put your friends and family first. Work can wait! Even mine,' Santa said with a wink.

With the Trundles' house being a little snug and Santa being jolly-normous, the big man practically filled every inch of the living room.

'H-h-hello, Santa!' Bob Trundle squeaked, as excited as ever to see his idol.

'Pamela! Bobalob! How marvellous it is to see you all. Has it really been a year already? My goodness, and look how much you two have grown! William and Brenda too! And where's that little doggy of yours –

Growler? Ah, there you are! *Ruff-woof-woff, ruffedy ruff-ruff, woof!*' Santa barked, and Growler hopped around like a little puppy.

'Santa, I never knew you could speak dog,' Brenda said.

'Of course I can! They don't call me Santa Paws for nothing. I'll teach you if you like. It's really quite simple; you just –'

'Santa! There's no time for barking lessons. Scrooge is on the loose and sucking the joy out of Christmas!' said William.

'Oh yes! Right you are. We'll bark on Boxing Day! Now, tell me what happened. Start at the very beginning, but skip the boring bits and . . . perhaps we should get a snack first?' Santa said hopefully, his giganterrific belly rumbling. 'I didn't quite manage to finish breakfast.'

'*Santa!*' William said impatiently.

'Oh yes, very well. Snacks afterwards, then.'

William explained everything – about the mysterious library appearing out of nowhere, the strange book following him home, waking up to Christmas destruction, and then all the anti-Christmas activity that had been blasted over the news ever since.

'We think he came out of *this*,' William said, handing Santa the ivy-green copy of *A Christmas Carol*.

'Oh, this is one of my favourite books! Ho, ho, I do love a spooky story!' Santa said, unable to resist flicking the book open. Without thinking, he began reading.

'*And yet that face of Marley, seven years dead, came* . . .'

'No, wait!' William cried, but it was too late – for as those words left Santa's lips, the book in his hands started to glow an eerie green.

'Oh dear,' Santa gasped when suddenly the see-through head of a ghost popped out of the page and looked around at them all.

'**ARRRGGHHHHHHH!**' everyone screamed as Santa dropped the book on the floor and the ghost flew out. This uninvited guest was just as spooky as you would imagine. There was no colour in him at all except grey, and I'm not sure that even counts as a colour. He had long, chunky chains wrapped all around him, which seemed to go on and on as he pulled them out of the pages.

'It's a g-g-GHOST!' Pamela squealed.

'That's not just any ghost . . . It's Jacob Marley!' Bob said, recognizing the spirit.

'The chains!' William cried. 'Don't let them leave the book or he'll escape!'

The Christmasaurus sprung to action, leapt across the room and slammed the book shut, just in time to trap the end of Marley's chains inside the glowing pages.

Marley didn't look happy about that. Not one bit!

Well, you can't blame him really, can you? If you were a spooky ghost wrapped in chains and stuck inside a book, I bet you'd be a bit grumpy too!

'Scroooooooge!' Marley's ghost called out in a terrifying wail.

'Oooh, he's a spooky fella!' Santa whispered. 'Maybe I don't like ghost stories after all!' And with that, he covered his eyes with his thick, fluffy beard and dived for cover behind the sofa, too scared to look at the ghost. 'Tell me when it's over!'

Bob and Pamela were next to get spooked out and quickly leapt after Santa to join him in his hiding spot. That just left William, Brenda and the Christmasaurus, who looked at each other and rolled their eyes. *Grown-ups are utterly useless sometimes!*

'Jacob Marley!' William called. 'Get back inside your story!'

But the ghost didn't listen. He carried on trying to escape from the pages, tugging on his chains. The Christmasaurus, however, held the book closed tight in his teeth.

'We've got to do something! We can't have *two* people

from this book on the loose! We need to get him back inside his story!' Brenda said, but the spirit pulled hard and started a phantasmic tug of war in the living room.

Marley pulled one way, and the ghost-busting trio pulled the other, smashing into the furniture and sending decorations flying as they all held on tight to the book.

CRASH! SMASH! CRACK!

'Not Christmas Tree Number Seven!' Bob groaned as the Christmasaurus's tail knocked the latest tree over, along with all the decorations.

I don't know if you've ever tried playing tug of war with a ghost and a dinosaur in your living room (I wouldn't recommend it!) but, let me tell you, it makes a mess . . . A **BIG** mess. In the tug-of-war chaos, baubles were crunched, the inflatable snowman was popped, and a musical snow globe smashed on the floor and started playing its tinkly little Christmas carol, which sounded totally creepy with a ghost whizzing around the room.

'Oh, I just can't bear it! It's all too spooky for me. Think happy thoughts! Think happy thoughts . . .' Santa said to himself, and he started humming along to the musical snow globe to distract himself from the creepy chaos.

All of a sudden, Marley stopped.

He stopped trying to escape, stopped wailing out for Scrooge, stopped tugging on his chains. The ghost just paused in the middle of the room as though he was listening to *something*, but the only sound in the room was the creaking carol from the cracked musical snow globe – and scaredy-cat Santa warbling along to it from his hiding place behind the sofa.

'What's Marley doing?' Brenda whispered.

'I don't know, but look at the decorations!' William said, noticing that it wasn't just the ghost that was acting strangely.

The bits of broken decorations were starting to

UNBREAK!

That's right! They were reversing!

The baubles unshattered, the inflatable snowman unpopped and all the Christmassy mess that the tug of war with Marley's ghost had made in the room started returning to normal.

'Look at the chains!' Brenda whispered, and William

168

realized that the links of Marley's heavy chains were starting to rattle, as if they were trying to get back inside the pages!

'Chrissy, let go!' William said, and the Christmasaurus quickly opened his mouth and dropped the book.

The cover flew open, allowing the chains of Marley's ghost to shoot back inside as though some invisible force was pulling them in.

Marley's ghost was now swirling around the room like he was being flushed down a toilet! William, Brenda and the Christmasaurus were more Ghostflushers than Ghostbusters as they watched Marley spin round and round, being sucked back inside his story.

'*ScrooooOOOOOOOGE!*' he wailed one final time as the remaining decorations fixed themselves, the last of which was the musical snow globe, which floated back up to its home on the mantelpiece just as its tinkly carol came to an end.

William, Brenda and the Christmasaurus watched Marley's ghost return to his story – and, as the last wisps of his chains disappeared within the pages, William slammed the book shut.

CHAPTER NINETEEN
A KITCHEN CAROL

With Marley's ghost firmly back inside *A Christmas Carol*, Bob did what all dads do in a crisis. He put the kettle on.

With fresh brews, hot chocolates and shortbread biscuits, they all sat around the kitchen table to calm their nerves and come up with a plan.

'Well, that was all a bit spooky, wasn't it?' Santa said with a mouthful of biscuit and a beardful of crumbs.

'Why did Marley's ghost go back into the book?' William asked Santa.

'Not the foggiest! I'm afraid this is far beyond anything I've ever seen before,' Santa said, carefully turning the green book over in his hands.

The icy scales running up the Christmasaurus's spine rose, and he backed away, growling warily.

'Don't worry, Chrissy,' said Santa. 'I'm definitely not reading anything from this book out loud again!'

'*Out . . . loud . . .*' William repeated as an idea started to form in his mind.

He turned to Santa.

'Do you remember when all the decorations were getting knocked over and the snow globe started playing that Christmas carol?' he asked.

'Oh yes, that tinkly little song was the only thing taking my mind off the ghost!' Santa replied, dunking his fifth shortbread in his cup of tea.

'Yes – and, Santa, you started singing along . . .' remembered Brenda.

'Well, I had to sing along to drown out the sound of old Marley wailing "*ScroooOOOOGE!*"' Santa did his best impression, then shuddered at the memory and took another two biscuits from the jar to calm himself.

'What are you thinking, Willypoos?' asked Bob, who

could sense the cogs in his son's mind ticking, as dads always can.

'Santa, you've always said that music is magical, right?' William said.

'Oh yes! Music is a magic like no other – it can do incredible, unexplainable things,' Santa said with a twinkle in his eyes. 'Music can make you feel happy when you're sad; it can make you want to get up and dance. It can remind us of people who are no longer with us, or send us off to faraway places . . .'

'Faraway, like . . . back inside a story?' William asked.

Everyone paused and looked at William as they started to understand what he was suggesting.

'I know it sounds impossible, but when the snow globe started playing that Christmas carol and Santa began to join in, Marley's ghost – *changed*,' William explained.

'Not just the ghost. All my decorations fixed themselves too!' Bob added.

'*A Christmas Carol*?' Santa whispered, reading the golden letters on the cover of the book.

'So, you think that to get Scrooge back inside the book we need to play him . . . Christmas carols?' Brenda asked, and by the look on her face she clearly had doubts about William's theory.

'Maybe!' said William.

'Hmmm.' Santa sighed. 'If only we had some way to test it out. Something from *their* world; something from inside their story.'

Suddenly Pamela shrieked with excitement, making the Christmasaurus leap into the air with fright. Then she sprinted out of the kitchen and disappeared down the hall.

'What the crackers was that all about?' Santa asked, but before anyone could guess, Pamela came practically skipping back into the room carrying something in her hands.

'How about *this*?' she said, laying down the two halves of Scrooge's broken walking cane on the table.

'Scrooge's cane!' cried Bob, smiling. 'He dropped it when he first came out of the book.'

'That's it!' William cheered.

'Righty-ho, let's test this theory of yours! Christmasaurus, fetch the snow globe!' Santa ordered, grabbing one last biscuit while the Christmasaurus collected the snow globe from the mantelpiece and carefully handed it to Santa.

'Let's see if you're right, William,' Santa said, turning the snow globe upside down and winding the little key in the bottom to make it play.

As the notes started tinkling the merry melody, Santa put the snow globe down and stepped back. Bob and Pamela took cover behind a kitchen chair while William and Brenda hid behind the Christmasaurus.

Nothing happened at first, but after a few seconds a little green spark fizzed across the cover of the book.

'Did you see that?' William gasped.

'My goodness, Willypoos, you were right!' Bob clapped excitedly as another spark zapped from the book.

'Why isn't the cane disappearing back inside it like Marley's ghost did, though?' Brenda said.

William had an idea. He wheeled himself out from behind the Christmasaurus and started singing along to the carol.

'We wish you a merry Christmas!
We wish you a merry Christmas!

We wish you a merry Christmas
and a happy new year . . .'

Suddenly the book threw open its cover as though William's voice had commanded it to do so.

'Ho-ho-ho, my goodness! It's working! Everybody sing!' Santa cried, and the whole family, including the Christmasaurus and Growler, started singing, roaring and howling together.

'Good tidings we bring
To you and your kin.
We wish you a merry Christmas
And a happy new year!'

As they sang, the music's magic started working.

First, the cane wibbled . . .

Then it wobbled . . .

Then it **wibbled and wobbled!**

The two halves lifted off the table and floated in the air. All of a sudden it clicked back together, with every tiny splintered bit of wood slotting perfectly into place like a jigsaw puzzle.

William felt the excitement in the kitchen grow and, as they belted out the final lines of the carol, a bolt of green energy zapped out of the open book. Fingers of electricity grabbed the cane and pulled it back inside.

The song ended and the cover whipped shut. The green glow faded, and the book lay still and quiet, looking like any ordinary old book.

'**IT WORKED!**' they all cheered together, and the Christmasaurus roared in celebration as everyone danced merrily around the room.

Then . . .

BREAKING NEWS!

The two red words suddenly flashed on the television screen and Stan Walker appeared.

'News just in: Buckingham Palace has released an official royal statement! *By order of the King of England: Christmas has been cancelled.*'

CHAPTER TWENTY
THE MAP TO SCROOGE

anta's knees wobbled at the breaking news announcement.

'*C-c-cancelled?*' he spluttered and coughed, big tears forming in his blue eyes, while Bob turned the volume up to listen to the latest report.

'With so many Christmas events disrupted – festive light switch-ons *switched off*, ice rinks melted, grottos forgotten – His Majesty, the King of England, made an unexpected announcement today,' Stan Walker said as the king's face appeared on the TV.

'Citizens of Great Britain, it has come to my attention what an utter waste of time this thing called Christmas is. I therefore feel it is my duty to intervene and order that it is cancelled immediately. Merry . . . I mean, *bah humbug,*' the king finished.

'*Bah humbug?* **BAH HUMBUG?!**' Bob shouted at the TV. 'Did you hear what the king said?'

'We all saw it, honey,' Pamela said, trying to calm Bob down.

'If Scrooge has got to the King of England, we might already be too late!' Brenda gasped, as an image of the royal Christmas tree appeared, being carried out of the palace by members of the King's Guard, and hoisted through the gates into a big bin.

As if that wasn't disturbing enough, the news then cut to images from around the country, where people were taking down Christmas lights, clearing away decorations and dumping their own trees.

They were abandoning Christmas!

There was a moment of silence in the room.

William realized he needed to snap everyone out of it.

THE MAP TO SCROOGE

'We are not giving up!' he cried. 'It's Christmas Eve, and if anyone can save Christmas, it's us! We just need to find Scrooge and get him back in that book, then everything else will fix itself too, like our decorations did!'

'But we don't even know where he is!' Brenda said.

'Well, actually, I have been tracking his movements,' Bob said as he carefully took the book and the snow globe off the kitchen table and flipped the tablecloth to reveal a hand-drawn map covered in little green dots.

'These dots represent everywhere that Scrooge has *de*-Christmassed so far,' Bob explained, pointing to the little green marks that he'd dotted all over the map.

There was a dot on their house for where Scrooge had first appeared, and another dot at the school, and dots on all the places that Bob had seen reported on the news.

'If we know where Scrooge has already been, maybe there's a clue on here about where he'll go next,' Bob added.

'Scrooge hates Christmas, so surely he'll be somewhere in the middle of nowhere, miles away from anything Christmassy,' Pamela suggested.

'Like up a mountain?' Brenda said, pointing to Mount Snowdon in Wales.

'Or out in the countryside perhaps?' Bob added, placing a finger on a forest in the middle of the country.

But, as William studied the dots of Scrooge sightings on the map, he realized something.

'I don't think Scrooge is running *away* from Christmas,' William said. 'All these Scrooge sightings are at super-Christmassy places: Oxford Street . . .'

'The panto . . .'

'Winter Wonderland . . .'

'This house!' Bob added, a little proudly.

'My goodness, you're right! He's not running away from Christmas at all,' Santa said.

'He's running *towards* it!' said William. 'And when he gets there, he *humbugs* it!'

'He *whats* it?' asked Pamela.

'*Humbugs!* You know – *bah humbug*. If Christmas carols spread Christmas cheer, then Scrooge's *bah humbugs* must do the opposite!' explained Brenda.

Pamela's eyes widened. 'So that's why people hear the whispering in the air!'

'Right! It's the last thing they hear before forgetting the joy of Christmas,' William added.

'I hate to burst your bauble. We might have figured out that Scrooge is hunting down Christmassy places, but that doesn't tell us where he'll be next,' Brenda pointed out.

William stared at the green dots . . .

'Wait,' he said. 'Maybe this map does show us the way. Look at Dad's green dots. Scrooge started out by travelling away from Holly Heath but the most recent dots, including Whiffington, show he's working his way back. But why?'

Suddenly the Christmasaurus went as giddy as a puppy, wagging his tail and scampering around the room to Santa.

'What is it, Chrissy, you daft dino?' Santa chuckled as the Christmasaurus stuffed his snout into Santa's giant pocket and pulled out a thick envelope.

'My letter!' William said, recognizing the envelope and the handwriting.

The Christmasaurus dropped it on William's lap and huffed through his nose: ***OPEN IT!***

A Christmasaurus Carol

William pulled out the letter he'd written to Santa just over a week ago. But the Christmasaurus huffed again at the envelope, and when William looked inside he remembered what else he'd sent them.

The Map to Scrooge

'The Holly Jolly Jinglers Carol Concert!' William said, pulling out the flyer that he'd sent along with his letter.

'That's it!' Bob cheered. 'There's no place more Christmassy on Christmas Eve than the Holly Jolly Jinglers Carol Concert!'

'Scrooge must have seen a poster for the concert when he was causing Christmas chaos at school,' Brenda gasped.

'Then that's where Scrooge will be!' Santa declared.

'And he's going try to *humbug* it,' Brenda said.

'If he does, then Christmas will be done for!' Bob whispered.

'Then we'd better be ready for him. We need to make this the most Christmassy Christmas carol concert in history!' William said.

'But how? All the Christmas lights are out, and people are taking down decorations as we speak. There's not even a Christmas tree in the town square any more!' Brenda said.

'If we only knew someone who had a seemingly endless supply of Christmas trees, who could lend a few to us . . .' Santa said, as all their eyes turned to Bob Back-Up-Tree Trundle.

A Christmasaurus Carol

'Dad, how many back-up trees do you actually have?' William asked.

A big grin stretched across Bob's face.

'I'll show you.'

CHAPTER TWENTY-ONE
BOB'S BACK-UP TREES

H ave you ever thought about collecting
something? Lots of people do.

Some people collect spoons. Not for eating.
Good heavens! No, these types of spoons will never
know the cool feel of a crisp scoop of ice cream or even
a dunk in a bowl of frosted flakes. No – a spoon collector
wouldn't dream of taking a spoon out of their special
spoon-display cabinet.

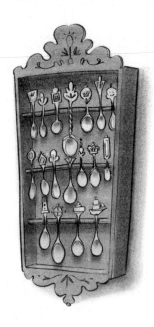

Other people collect stamps. You know, the little square sticky things that go in the corner of an envelope. Except these stamp collectors won't ever post a letter with them. No, no, no! These are stamps for keeping in special folders on a special shelf (or in a box in the loft!).

Some people collect toys they'll never play with, cars they'll never drive or instruments they'll never rock. The list of collections is wonderfully odd and endlessly fun, and . . . I bet you're wondering why I'm telling you all this! Well, Bob Trundle had an odd collection of his own. A secret collection that only he knew about.

Bob's secret collection was, as I'm sure you've guessed, motorbikes . . .

KIDDING!

Bob collected **CHRISTMAS TREES** (of course!).

Now, you're probably thinking, *How on earth can someone collect Christmas trees? How many has he got, and where does he keep them all?* – and these are all the exact same questions that William and the Christmas gang were thinking too.

Luckily for them, and for us, Bob was about to give them the answer.

'Follow me!' Bob said excitedly, as he moved towards the hallway, where he stopped and turned to face everyone.

'What I'm about to show you is top secret,' he

announced, with a dramatic twinkle in his eye.

'Oh, get on with it, darling. Christmas isn't going to save itself!' Pamela yelled.

'All right, all right!' Bob said, opening the door to the cupboard under the stairs and stepping inside, totally disappearing into the darkness within.

Santa, the Christmasaurus, Pamela, Brenda and William all looked at each other, wondering where Bob had gone.

CLICK!

A light flicked on.

Actually, it was about ten thousand twinkly fairy lights that illuminated a rather large hole in the wall, which led straight into the garage!

'You knocked a hole in the wall!' Pamela squeaked.

'Well, it was tricky carrying the Christmas decorations from the garage through the back garden and into the house,' Bob explained.

'Trickier than knocking a hole in the wall?!' Brenda questioned.

'Are you cross about the wall?' Bob asked Pamela a little nervously.

BOB'S BACK-UP TREES

'Cross? **I LOVE IT**!' Pamela beamed. 'You're like a Christmas superhero and we've just found your secret lair. A bit like the Batcave.'

'**The Bobcave!**' Santa boomed.

'A superhero? That's the nicest thing anyone's ever said to me,' Bob said, going red.

They all leant into the cupboard to take a good look around the Bobcave, and William saw that not only had Bob knocked through the wall but he'd given the garage a makeover too.

The garage used to be full of rusty tools, William's old wheelchair parts and bits of things that didn't seem to belong to anything. But not any more. No: this was bright, clean and **VERY MERRY**!

'There's a place for everything. Come in – let me give you a tour! I like to call this area *Bauble Lane*.' Bob grinned, pulling out drawer after drawer to reveal colour-coordinated baubles.

'And this is my custom tinsel dispenser. We stock both shiny **AND** glittery.' He beamed with pride as he unravelled a length of shimmering tinsel.

'And over here we have fairy lights, indoor and

outdoor! I keep our wreaths up on these hooks. That's my cabinet of candy canes. Those shelves are just for elves. We've got hangers for stockings, padded cases for snow globes, and all other decorations are stored in alphabetical order, from angels to Xmas, yule logs and . . . well, there's not much in the Z compartment.'

'My goodness, you've been a busy Bob, haven't you?' Santa said in admiration.

'And you've not seen the best part – my tree collection!' Bob said.

He started winding a lever on the wall, which was connected to a rope of tinsel that pulled back a sparkly curtain to reveal a collection of Christmas trees, all squeezed together like a small (a very small) festive forest, right there in the Trundles' garage.

'**Ta-da!**' Bob beamed.

Santa laughed. 'Ho, ho! Perfect, Bobalob! We can use these to trap old Scroogey-pants and buy us enough time to Christmas-carol him back into *A Christmas Carol*!'

'How many trees are there, Dad?' William asked, looking at the nice but small collection, trying to imagine them all spread out around the town square.

'Well, I had twenty, but we've lost quite a few since then so thirteen now, I think.' Bob sighed, thinking of his fallen trees.

'Thirteen? But . . . the town square is huge!' Brenda said. 'They might fill up our little garage, but you'd hardly notice thirteen trees in the square!'

'She's right,' William said. 'If we want to distract Scrooge for long enough to carol him back into that book, we're going to need more than that. Sorry, Dad.'

DING-DONG!

At that very moment, the doorbell rang.

'Who could that be?' wondered Pamela.

The Christmasaurus growled, sniffing the air, then screwed up his face as if he'd smelt a rotten sprout.

'What is it, Chrissy?' William asked.

'He's picked up a bad whiff,' Santa explained.

'A *whiff*? Of course! Perfect timing!' Bob said, rubbing his hands together excitedly as he ran back through the hole in the wall, past the family, to answer the front door, where a bin man and a young girl whom William instantly recognized from the TV were waiting.

'You're Lucy, the girl from the dump,' said William, as he joined his dad at the door. 'We saw you on the telly!'

'Oh, yeah, that's me,' Lucy said, her cheeks going a little red with embarrassment. 'And that's my dad, Larry,' she added, pointing to her dad, who was standing behind her.

BOB'S BACK-UP TREES

'We've got some trees for the Christmas-tree collector,' said Larry, and everyone glanced over his shoulder at the rubbish collection truck that was overflowing with unwanted Christmas trees from Whiffington.

Bob smiled. 'You've come to the right place!'

Chapter Twenty-Two
SCROOGE TRAP

It was already getting late on Christmas Eve and time was running out to save Christmas from being *Scroogefied*. BUT, with the Whiffington trees and two extra helpers – Lucy and Larry – the plan was suddenly simple.

'*STEP ONE!*' William called, and everyone gathered around to listen to the plan. 'We take as many Christmas trees and decorations as we can down to the town square.'

'We can use the sleigh to fly it all there!' Santa said. 'Perfect!'

Everyone nodded in agreement.

'**STEP TWO!** We make the town square look like the Christmassiest Christmas party on the planet. We won't have long, so, Dad, we'll need your best decorating skills!'

'Yes, sir! I mean, yes, *son*!' Bob saluted.

'**STEP THREE!** We meet the Holly Jolly Jinglers at the bandstand for the ultimate Holly Jolly Jingling Christmas Carol Concert! This is the part that's going to get Scrooge back into the book, so it has to be perfect!' William said.

'But what if these Holly Jolly Jingly people don't show up? What if they've been humbugged too?' Lucy asked.

'Nothing will stop the Holly Jolly Jinglers. They won't let us down!' Bob replied confidently.

'Oh, and don't forget **STEP FOUR**, when we all get to hear you sing your solo, Willypoos!' Bob added, beaming.

'Solo?' Brenda narrowed her eyes at William, and he remembered how she'd stared at him when he'd told his dad about getting the solo, and how she had been able to sense that he'd been lying. Quickly, he elbowed her so that she wouldn't say any more. He knew he needed to tell his dad the truth. He just wasn't ready to tell him yet.

'So,' Bob said, 'the Jinglers sing their carol, William sings his solo, then **BAM!** The spirit of Christmas will be so overpowering that Scrooge will be blasted back inside his story, and all the joy he humbugged away will return to the world! Santa will deliver his presents and, *Bob's your uncle*, Christmas will be saved!'

'No, Bob's my *dad*.' William smiled as they all got to work.

The gang didn't waste a second and started gathering seasonal supplies from Bob's secret stash. They quickly reached the first hurdle in this plan – transportation issues!

'You call that a sleigh?! What happened to the proper one?' Brenda frowned, looking up towards the roof at Santa's Other Sleigh. It was clearly WAY too small for the cargo they needed to shift. Santa could barely fit in it, let alone all the decorations from Bob's garage and the trees from Whiffington!

'The elves are loading the main sleigh full of toys,

of course!' Santa explained. 'I had to use the back-up sleigh.'

'Did someone say back-up? Here's the first!' said Bob, dragging a Christmas tree across the front garden before gawping up at the cool yet tiny sleigh on the roof.

'You can use our rubbish truck, Mr Claus! Right, Dad?' Lucy said, looking up a little nervously at Larry.

'Of course! Plenty of room – you'll fit everything you need in there!' Larry agreed, taking off his hat and bowing his head at the big man.

'That's a jolly marvellous idea! Lucy Dungston . . . ah, yes, I remember you. You've always been a solid Nice Lister! A few creaky floorboards in your house, though. Makes it a little tricky not waking you up.' Santa smiled as they began adding Bob's collection to the sparkling Whiffington donations in the back of the big green rubbish truck.

They made a long line from the garage to the truck and passed the decorations along, one by one, from Growler at one end to the Christmasaurus at the other. Tree after tree, bauble after bauble – the whole lot went in!

It was festive teamwork at its finest, with everyone working together until there wasn't a single speck of glitter left in the garage.

'Next stop, Holly Heath town square!' Bob said as he climbed into the passenger seat of the truck, while Larry started the engine.

That's when they hit the next hurdle in their plan.

BANG!

One of the truck's tyres blew.

'It's all the Christmas trees! We're too heavy!' said Larry. 'It's OK, though – it's only one tyre. We can still make it as long as we don't lose any more.'

Well, I bet you can guess what happened the moment Larry said that . . .

BANG!

Yep, another tyre blew, and the metal rims of the truck's wheels sank into the slushy snow in the road.

'NO!' William cried.

'It's too heavy!' Lucy said.

'Well, this isn't good, not good at all! If we can't budge this truck and decorate the square, then Scrooge will barely have to utter one *humbug* and he'll win, just like that. Ebenezy-peasy!' Santa said, scratching his beard as he searched for a solution.

'There must be a way,' Brenda said, as Bob and Larry climbed down from the truck, looking defeated.

'I'm sorry, but that truck isn't moving an inch with two flat tyres unless it sprouts wings and flies out of here!' Larry said.

At those words, the Christmasaurus suddenly leapt to his scaly feet, as though someone had zapped him with a bolt of lightning.

'What is it, Chrissy?' Santa asked.

'Whatever Larry just said gave him an idea!' William explained, somehow knowing exactly what was going on in the Christmasaurus's mind.

'Something I just said?' Larry asked. 'But I said that truck won't move an inch with two flat tyres!'

'*Unless* . . .' William added, remembering what Larry had said after that.

The Christmasaurus galloped over to the large rubbish truck and positioned himself in front of it, standing tall and firm in the slush, his tail straight and his head low, like he was ready.

'Unless what?' Larry said, totally baffled.

'Unless the truck does exactly what you suggested.' William smiled with an excited sparkle in his eye. 'It flies!'

CHAPTER TWENTY-THREE
FLYING RUBBISH

The plan had changed.

With two flat tyres, there was only one way of getting that truckload of Christmas stuff over to the town square – **by air**. And there was only one creature magical enough to pull it.

'Fly? It's not designed to fly!' Larry said, pacing around and scratching his head.

'So, you're saying that dino of yours can pull this truck like reindeer pull Santa's sleigh?' Lucy asked William, looking totally confused.

'Exactly!' William replied.

'Don't worry, I didn't believe it at first either,' Brenda

added, as Santa and the Trundle gang worked together to harness the Christmasaurus to the front of the enormous rubbish truck. Lucy and her dad got to work, securing the trees for air travel.

'Are you sure you can do this? It's a lot bigger than the sleigh and there's only one of you!' William whispered to his blue scaly friend while the others were busy.

The Christmasaurus merely huffed back at him through his nostrils, and William understood what he was saying straight away: *Believe!*

'I *do* believe in you, of course I do!' William quickly replied. William knew all about the power of belief. It was what made the Christmasaurus fly like Santa's reindeer in the first place, and if there was even a shadow of doubt from any of them tonight, then there would be zero chance of this one brave dinosaur whizzing that **HUGE-NORMOUS** truck across the sky.

'The truck's secure and ready to fly . . . I think!' Lucy shouted from the back of the vehicle.

'We'd better get airborne fast – the weather's turning,' Santa said, looking up at the clouds that had begun swirling overhead. They weren't just any clouds; they were the grumbliest grey clouds William had ever seen, covering the whole sky like a blanket of pure misery.

'There's only one person with a heart so devoid of happiness that it could conjure up a sky like this on Christmas Eve!' Santa said.

'Scrooge is getting more powerful, isn't he?' William asked, looking up.

Santa sighed. 'I'm afraid so. Christmas Eve should be covered in twinkly snow, not dreary, miserable clouds. He's not only sucking the Christmas spirit out of people, but out of the air itself!'

'Then let's get Christmas cracking!' Bob shouted like a battle cry.

'Righteo, Bob. All aboard then!' Santa said, holding the door open as though he expected everyone to somehow magically squeeze inside.

'Sorry, Santa, it's just too small for everyone to fit in here,' Larry said.

'Too small? We'll have to do something about that!' Santa smiled as he rolled up his red sleeves, like he was getting ready to lift something heavy.

'Are you going to do some magic?' Lucy asked excitedly.

'Magic? Ho-ho-no. I'm not a wizard! No, no, this is more of a science experiment,' he said, as he started twiddling his fingers through the air. 'I'm simply manipulatwingling the jolliocity of the partycols of the truck so that they magniferify. It's fairly straight-forward, really; any elf can do this.' Santa shrugged, as though what he said made total sense, but obviously it all sounded just as ridiculous to them as it probably does to you.

The Christmasaurus rolled his blue eyes and grunted an explanation to William.

'Oh! What Santa is trying to do is make the truck bigger!' William translated.

'Precisely! Only . . .' Santa frowned, as though trying to solve a complicated equation.

'Only what?' Brenda asked.

'Well, it's just that I've only ever manipulatwingled chimneys, expanding them so that I can squeeze into them with all those presents! But I'm sure this'll be no problem! No problem at all. Move back!'

They all moved back and waited. William watched as Santa focused his energy towards the truck.

FLYING RUBBISH

There was silence.

Then a bit more silence.

Then the silence got quieter.

'What's meant to happen?' Brenda whispered to William.

'I don't know!' William hissed back.

'Well, what happens when he does this on chimneys?'

William thought about it, trying to remember what it was like when Santa enlarged the chimneys.

'One minute they're normal and then suddenly, out of nowhere, everything just gets . . .'

William paused. His mouth fell open in total disbelief.

'. . . bigger!' He gawped, pointing through the door of the Whiffington rubbish truck.

On the outside, not much had changed. It still looked like Larry Dungston's truck, but through the door, the gang could see that the inside had somehow stretched and expanded so that there was enough room for everyone to fit comfortably inside.

'I don't believe it!' Pamela whispered.

'Ho-ho! It worked!' Santa beamed. 'I only had time to manipulatwingle the inside, I'm afraid, but it's not bad for my first non-chimney expansion. Not bad at all! Climb aboard then!'

Larry got in first, staring around the spacious cabin, which was now many times bigger than before, and had extra space for boxes of decorations. Lucy climbed in next, followed by Pamela and Brenda, then Bob.

'Oh, and if my manipulatwingulations were correct, there should be one more little modification,' Santa said, as he gave the truck a gentle kick with his boot and a ramp unfolded in front of William's chair.

'Thanks, Santa.' William smiled as he wheeled himself inside the cabin and Santa closed the door behind him.

'Aren't you coming in?' William asked Santa, who was still outside, standing next to the expanded vehicle.

'No-no, I'm in the pilot seat!' Santa winked as he clambered up on to the roof of the truck and parked his bum right over their heads. (Thankfully there wasn't a sun roof, or those below would've got a bit of a shock!)

'All right, time for some musical magic! William, you know what to do!' Santa boomed from above.

'Right! Lucy, have you got any Christmas songs?' William asked.

'Of course! It's all me and Dad listen to on our rubbish runs in December!' Lucy said, switching on the truck's old CD player.

'So that's why you haven't been *humbugged* by Scrooge!' Bob realized, as merry Christmas music filled the cabin and leaked out of the windows into the frosty air, like heat from a radiator warming up a cold room.

'Ho, ho! That's like music to my ears!' Santa cheered.

'It *is* music to your ears!' Bob called up, and everyone laughed.

Suddenly the truck lifted a little off the slushy road and bobbed like a ball floating on water.

'What was that?' Lucy asked, grabbing hold of her seat.

William smiled at her. 'That's the magic of music!'

'You ain't seen nothin' yet! Over to you, Chrissy!' Santa cried from above, and they all looked out at the Christmasaurus, who dug his claws into the slush and began to pull.

At first, nothing seemed to happen. It was as if the Christmasaurus was trying to pull a mountain.

'It's impossible!' Lucy said.

'It *is* impossible if you think it is,' William said. 'You all need to believe.'

'We need more than that to get this truck in the air! You need magic, not belief!' Larry scoffed.

'No, belief *is* the magic!' William explained, as they all watched the Christmasaurus, who was trying his best to heave the heavy load down the road.

'I believe!' Pamela said.

Suddenly the truck jolted forward.

'Me too! Obviously!' Brenda added, and the truck lurched again.

It was starting to work!

'I believe in you, Christmasaurus!' Bob said, cheering triumphantly, making the truck start to slide down the street.

In the driveway of the Trundle house, Growler let out a howl as he watched the truck move away. He might not have been able to join them in the rubbish truck, but he could help by believing in the magical dinosaur too!

The Christmasaurus started to pick up speed like a plane on a runway.

Bob looked to Larry. It was his turn.

'I guess there's nothing to lose. You can do it, dino! I believe!' Larry called out of the window, and **whoosh**! The Christmasaurus was now starting to stride across the slush.

'Well?' William said to Lucy.

'If it means I get to see a dinosaur flying across the sky, I'll believe in anything! I BELIEVE!' Lucy shouted, and the sound of the Christmasaurus's claws clopping on the street fell silent, for he was now galloping on the air itself.

There was just one person left in the truck to say it. The most important person of all – for without William's belief, the Christmasaurus would never have flown in the first place.

William wound down the window on the passenger side, stuck his head out and yelled at the top of his voice:

'I BELIEVE IN YOU, CHRISTMASAURUS!'

The moment those words landed in the Christmasaurus's ears, it was as though someone had given him a turboboost of Christmas energy.

SWOOOSH!

They were in the air and zooming along the street.

**'Over the rooftops, away we fly,
On to adventure, into the sky!'**

Santa sang from his
makeshift pilot's seat up
top as the Christmasaurus
pulled the entire
rubbish truck and its
Christmas cargo
up to the clouds.

CHAPTER TWENTY-FOUR

DROPPING DECORATIONS

Have you ever peeped through your curtains on Christmas Eve and looked up, hoping to catch a glimpse of Santa flying across the sky?

If you have, I bet you were hoping to see a sleigh loaded with toys and presents being pulled by glorious, galloping reindeer, right?

Well, any children in Holly Heath who decided to peep through their curtains on this Christmas Eve would have had the shock of their lives! Because, instead of a sleigh, they would have spotted a grubby green rubbish truck overflowing with decorations, soaring across the stars, with Santa perched on the roof and clinging on to reins that were harnessed to a big blue **DINOSAUR**!

It was a brilliantly bizarre sight, and of all the wild adventures William had been on with his friend the Christmasaurus, this was shaping up to be top of the list!

'WOOHOO!'

William cheered, sticking his head out of the truck window like an excited dog being driven down a motorway.

The Christmasaurus responded with a huge loop-the-loop, making the wheels of the truck skim the clouds.

'Ho-ho-ho!' Santa chortled from up top, loving every twist and turn.

'I shouldn't have eaten that packet of mince pies on the way from Whiffington!' Larry said, his face turning a deep shade of sprout green.

'This is **AWESOME**!' Lucy and Brenda cried as the truck looped upside down once more, making their hair stick up on end.

'Look, there's the town square!' Bob said, pointing out of the window at the streets ahead.

'It all looks so . . . *normal!*' William sighed, looking at the undecorated homes. 'It's Christmas Eve, but it might as well be the middle of March. There's not a bauble in sight!'

Brenda peered out of the window. 'But how *are* we going to decorate the square? A living room is one thing, but an entire town square?'

William thought for a moment, then smiled. 'We do it from up here! A Christmas **AIRDROP**! With the Christmasaurus taking us round, it'll be done in a jiffy. But – ah! Everything we need is in the back . . .'

Suddenly Santa's big bushy beard appeared at the driver's-side window. 'I hear you might be wanting these?' He grinned and passed a box of baubles through the window.

'Brilliant!' said William. 'Thanks, Santa! D'you think you could reach into the back and pass us more decorations?'

Santa beamed. 'No problem!'

And so Santa handed them bauble after bauble, light

after light, until the cabin was so jam-packed that it was like a Christmas cracker fit to burst.

'Oh-ho-ho!' exclaimed Santa. 'I do believe we have reached our destination!' he said, as he wiggled his bottom back into his spot on the roof. 'It's time to get down to business! Nice and low and take it slow-ho-ho, Chrissy!'

DROPPING DECORATIONS

Santa pulled on the reins as he steered the Christmasaurus towards the town square at the heart of Holly Heath.

'We're lined up straight
and ready to decorate . . .'

Goodness me, I've started rhyming like the elves!' Santa laughed, but the Christmasaurus remained focused on his task and pulled the enormous truck onwards through the air.

'It's over to you, Bob!' Santa called down.

'Me?' Bob squeaked nervously, his face turning as white as snow.

'Of course! When it comes to Christmas decorations, no one compares to the legendary Bob Trundle!' said Santa.

'*Legendary?* Did Santa just call me legendary?' asked Bob, unable to suppress his smile.

Larry grinned. 'Yeah, I think he did, mate!'

'It's time to put those decorating skills to good use!' said Pamela, beaming at Bob.

221

William smiled. 'All those hours you've spent carefully repositioning the tree to get the perfect angle . . .'

'And all those *endless* trips to the garden centre to pick up the perfect colour of tinsel!' Brenda added.

'Everything's just been practice for tonight. This is it. The big one, Dad. Your Christmas decorations could literally save Christmas!' said William, hoping his words would fill Bob with enough confidence to pull off **the most CHRISTMASSY** Christmas decorating session of all time.

'Do you really mean it?' Bob said, blushing.

'YES!' everyone cried.

'OK then . . . It's time to tinsel this town!' Bob said, as he rolled up the sleeves of his festive jumper.

'Let's see how much I've taught you. What's the first rule of Christmas decorating, Brenda?' Bob asked.

'I can't believe I know this . . . *Always start with the Christmas lights!*' Brenda said, shaking her head with embarrassment.

'CORRECT!'

Bob grinned with pride.

Dropping Decorations

'I've got the lights!' said Lucy, clutching a long roll of colourful Christmas lights.

'Perfect! Now, where to hang them? Let's see . . . A-ha, Right there! We'll wrap them round all the lamp posts and surround the square.' Bob pointed at a lamp post on the corner of the square. 'Do you think you could loop those lights round that one?' he asked Lucy.

'**Absolutely!**' replied Lucy, grabbing a pair of what appeared to be swimming goggles out of the glove compartment and pulling them over her eyes.

Brenda and William exchanged a confused look.

'I always wear safety goggles on adventures,' Lucy explained with a smile.

'I like her!' Brenda whispered to William as they watched Lucy tie a knot at the end of the string of lights, making a lasso, which she then dangled out of the window.

'I like her too!' said William.

'Steady now, Chrissy!' Santa called from the pilot seat as Lucy started to swing the string of lights round, as if she were a cowgirl.

'Here it comes!' said Bob as the Christmasaurus swooped the truck down nice and low.

'One . . .

two . . .

three . . .

NOW!'

Bob cried.

Lucy threw the Christmas lights down and lassoed the lamp post.

Everyone cheered, clapped and whooped as the Christmasaurus galloped in mid-air around the town square, swooping from lamp post to lamp post while Lucy, William and Brenda hooked the long string of Christmas lights round each one they passed, until the whole square was done.

Dropping Decorations

'Great job, team!' Bob said. 'Now we need some trees!'

'Leave that to me!' said Larry, reaching for a button on the dashboard that was labelled **RUBBISH RELEASE**. 'Just tell me when!' he said to Bob.

'Look! That's where the carol concert is going to be!' William exclaimed, pointing at the bandstand – a small stage in the centre of the square.

'Then we need to make that as Christmassy as your dad's jumper!' Larry said with a smile.

'Santa! Can you fly us over the bandstand?' Bob called out of the window.

'Say no more!' Santa said, grinning, and he steered the Christmasaurus towards the stage.

'Hold it . . . Hold it . . . ' Bob said, watching from the window. **'RELEASE THE TREES!'** he commanded.

Larry pushed the button and the doors to the rubbish container opened, releasing all the pre-decorated, fully lit Christmas trees they had loaded earlier.

Maybe it was their bushy branches acting like some sort of bristly parachute or perhaps a bit of Christmas magic at work, but whatever it was, every single tree somehow fell the right way up, landing perfectly on to the snowy ground below with a **THUD** and a **JINGLE**, like giant Christmas tree darts! **'Bullseye!'** Santa cheered as he watched the square below become more and more Christmassy.

Next came the baubles, which William, Brenda and Lucy threw in handfuls out of the

windows of the soaring truck, making it look as though it was raining giant glittery balls of every colour over Holly Heath.

'Now I get why you like decorating so much – this is awesome!' said Brenda, beaming at Bob. She handed him a shiny star-shaped tree-topper, which he threw over his shoulder without even looking – and they all watched as it landed **perfectly** on top of a tree.

William smiled. 'And *that's* why Santa said you're a legend!'

A Christmasaurus Carol

The Christmasaurus continued to fly in circuits round the square, while everyone in the truck threw out every decoration they had. All of Bob's collection, every piece of the Whiffington waste donations – not a single speck of sparkle was wasted!

Brenda gazed at the bandstand. 'I don't see any Holly Jolly Jinglers,' she said, giving William a nervous look.

'Don't worry. They won't let us down!' William said with certainty. 'We're still early and if the Jinglers say they'll be there at three o'clock then they'll be there at three o'clock!' But he couldn't help staring out of the window at the bandstand a little longer than everyone else, wishing for a glimpse of one of his choir friends.

Suddenly a red light began flashing on the dashboard of the truck.

'What does that mean?' William asked.

'That means the truck's empty!' Lucy explained.

'Then I think we'd better land and take a look,' Bob said nervously.

Santa steered the Christmasaurus down to the high street that ran alongside the square and they landed with a gentle bump.

DROPPING DECORATIONS

'**Whoa-ho-ho!**' Santa called, instructing the Christmasaurus to slow down.

Their dino-pilot instantly dug his claws into the icy road, sending up a spray of glistening snow into the air. It covered the windows of the truck, so all William and the rest of the gang could see was a sparkly wall of white, leaving them wondering if their decorations had worked . . .

Was it Christmassy enough to stop Scrooge in his tracks?

CHAPTER TWENTY-FIVE

CANCELLED CAROLS

All was quiet in the cramped Whiffington rubbish-collection truck as everyone waited nervously to see the result of their aerial decoration drop.

'Well, bless my baubles! It's more Christmassy than the North Pole!' William heard Santa's muffled voice mutter from up above.

There was a huge **SQUEEEEEEEAK** as Santa slid off the front of the truck and down the windscreen, wiping a bum-shaped gap through the frost – and revealing the newly decorated winter wonderland they had just created.

'Wow!' everyone said in unison as they admired their work.

Tinsel hung from every bristle of every tree, and strings of multicoloured lights twinkled on lamp posts. There were baubles of every colour of the rainbow all around, and candy canes seemed to dangle from anything they could possibly dangle from.

Most impressive of all, though, was the way the unwanted Christmas trees from Whiffington and Bob's back-up trees had landed perfectly to create a winding path through the square, leading right to the bandstand in the centre.

'The town square has never **EVER** looked this Christmassy! **You did it, Dad!**' cried William, glowing with pride.

'We all did it!' Bob said with a warm smile.

'I hate to burst your bauble, but it's not over yet!' Brenda interrupted. 'There's still a Christmas-hating fictional character from a magical book on the loose, trying to destroy Christmas!'

She pointed to the sky, which was the total opposite to the magical square they were in.

It was full of grim grey
clouds that were close
to bursting with humbug
misery, threatening to rain
down on the world below.

'Right you are, Brenda!' Santa said as he
unharnessed the Christmasaurus. 'If old Scroogey-pants
wants to humbug away all
things Christmassy, then he
won't be able to resist this
magical little spot we've made.
I reckon it won't be long until he
heads this way.'

'And right into our Scrooge trap!'
William cheered. 'It's time for
STEP THREE of the plan:

Assemble the Holly Jolly Jinglers!

They'll be arriving soon for the concert. That way, Christmasaurus! To the bandstand!' William cried, and his dinosaur friend leapt behind his wheelchair and used his scaly head to push him at dino-speed along the new path that wound its way through the freshly decorated Christmas-tree maze until they arrived at the bandstand, which was still deserted.

The bandstand was an octagonal structure with a pointed roof, no walls and a small stage, which, thanks to their decoration drop, was now covered in shiny sparkly things that made it glisten and glimmer against the grizzly grey sky overhead.

'Ah, this is the perfect spot for a Christmas Eve carol concert,' Santa said as they made their way on to the raised stage. 'Although, are you sure we've got the right time, young William? I can't see that anyone else is coming.'

'This is the place all right. Look at the banner,' Lucy said, pointing at a large banner attached to the side of the bandstand that said:

THE
HOLLY JOLLY JINGLERS
CAROL CONCERT
CHRISTMAS EVE 3 P.M.

'Three o'clock? That's only half an hour away!' Pamela said, looking at the large clock tower on the church across the square.

'They'll be here, trust me. The Jinglers wouldn't let us down,' Bob said confidently.

'Unless . . .' Brenda began nervously. 'Unless they think the concert has been cancelled.' Her face went pale as she raised her finger at the banner. As if by some sort of dark magic, gruesome green letters had suddenly appeared on it. Letters that spelled a word, just one word, scrawled over the banner so that it now said . . .

THE
HOLLY JO[LL]Y [JINGL]ERS
CANCELLED
[CHRIST]MAS EVE 3 P.M.

'Was that there before?' William asked, panicking.

'I . . . I . . . I don't know!' Bob spluttered.

'I didn't see it,' Pamela said.

'I think maybe there was something . . . ' Lucy said uncertainly.

'It's been **humbugged**!' Brenda yelled.

'But how? It makes no sense,' Larry muttered, scratching his head.

'I'm afraid it makes perfect sense,' said Santa. 'If Scrooge can leave his story, there's nothing to stop him from changing this one.'

'You mean, he's rewriting his own ending?' Bob cried.

'Bingo, Bob! Scrooge is no longer in his world, a world where he was destined to be visited by spirits of Christmases past, present and future, and confront his fears. He's in this one. *This* is his story now, and he's trying to create a new ending for himself, one where he can carry on being as miserable as he likes until the final page,' Santa explained.

The Christmasaurus started pacing around, sniffing the air. Time was running out!

'But without the Jinglers there'll be no concert.

Without the concert there'll be no singing . . . and without singing we'll have no way of carolling Scrooge back into his story and . . . and . . .' William trailed off as he realized that the end of Christmas was in sight.

'It's OK! We don't need *all* the Jinglers!' Bob said with a smile. 'We only need one. The most important one: **the soloist**! And we just so happen to have him right here – our very own **Jingling Willypoos**!'

He beamed with pride at his son, but William's heart sank in his chest.

He still hadn't told his dad the truth – that he hadn't really been selected to sing the solo at the carol concert. But there was no hiding from it any longer. It was time to come clean.

'Dad,' William mumbled, not looking his dad in the eye.

'It's OK if you're nervous, Willypoos! I was nervous too when I sang my first solo right here on this very spot!' Bob said.

'No. It's not that . . . Dad, I haven't been totally honest with you.' William gulped, then he took a deep breath, closed his eyes and just told his dad everything as quickly as he could, hoping it would be easier if he did it fast, like ripping off a plaster, and this is what he said (try to read this as quickly as you can, all in one breath, and it still won't be as fast as William said it!):

'*I didn't get the solo because Eddie Shepherd sang before me and he was so good, you should have heard him, and then I was too nervous to even try out. I couldn't even put my hand up and then it was too late, and then the book from the strange library followed me home and there wasn't the right moment to tell you the truth about the solo before Scrooge escaped from the story and started destroying Christmas, and the solo just slipped my mind until right now . . .*'

William finished and took another deep breath. (And you probably should too!)

Bob paused and looked at him for a moment. William was unsure if he was going to be upset.

'I'm sorry I let you down, Dad. I just wanted to be a Jolly Jingler like you, so you'd be proud of me,' said William.

Suddenly Bob threw his arms around his son.

'Willypoos, you don't have to be sorry. I don't care if you got the solo or not!'

'You don't?' said William.

'No! I just want you to be happy, and I'm even more proud of you for being honest.'

'Eventually!' Brenda added with a wink.

'Don't you think it's about time you were honest too, Bob?' Pamela said, raising her eyebrows.

'Honest about what?' William asked his dad, and Bob started nervously fidgeting.

'Oh, *this* is going to be good!' Santa whispered to the Christmasaurus as he perched his bottom on a bench next to the dinosaur, as if they were watching a Christmas movie.

'Well . . . I wasn't exactly given the solo when I was a

Jingler,' Bob said, going red with embarrassment.

'What do you mean? I thought you sang the solo on your first year as a Holly Jolly Jingler?' Brenda said.

'Yes, yes! And I did sing the solo but only because . . . because my mate Frank forgot all the words halfway through the first verse,' Bob confessed. 'He just **froze** with the whole town watching! So I leapt forward and –'

'Saved the day!' William cheered.

'Sounds more like he stole poor Frank's solo, if you ask me,' Brenda teased.

'So . . . I wasn't actually chosen. In fact, I was too scared to even volunteer!' Bob admitted.

'Just like me,' William whispered.

'Just like you!' said Bob.

'Why didn't you tell me that in the first place, Dad?' asked William.

'I guess . . . I just wanted you to be proud of me too.' Bob gave him a nervous smile.

Santa blew his nose into a red hanky as he and the Christmasaurus sobbed into each other's arms (and claws!).

'Are they always like this?' Lucy whispered to Brenda, eyeing Santa and his dino friend curiously.

'Lucy, you have no idea,' Brenda replied.

'Um, I hate to break up this lovely moment, but it'll be three o'clock in ten minutes and we still don't have one of these Holly Jolly Janglers,' Larry said.

'**JINGLERS!**' William and Bob corrected him together.

'But you were right, Dad,' added William. 'We do only need one Jingler – it just isn't me! We need Eddie Shepherd!'

'But if Scrooge has made Eddie think the concert is cancelled, then he'll be at home and that could be anywhere in Holly Heath!' Pamela said.

'If only **someone** knew where all the girls and boys in town lived . . .' said Brenda, loud enough for Santa to snap out of his sobbing.

'Wait a minute . . . *I* know where Eddie Shepherd lives! I've been there on this night every year since he was born! Let me think . . . Number twenty-six Cobble Avenue, the one with the red bricks!' said Santa, and just like that a new plan was made.

'It's time for a new Step Three of the plan,' William said. '**FIND EDDIE SHEPHERD!**'

CHAPTER TWENTY-SIX

FINDING THE JINGLER!

The race was on to find Eddie Shepherd and bring him to the town square so he could use his angelic voice to Christmas carol Scrooge back into the book he came from.

'Christmasaurus, can you fly me to Eddie's house?' William said.

The Christmasaurus didn't need asking twice. He hopped to his claws, pulled down a long string of extra-strong tinsel from the closest tree and used his teeth to wrap it securely round William's wheelchair. Then he wound the tinsel round his own scaly body like a sparkly harness and got into take-off position.

'You all wait here, and Chrissy and I will bring Eddie back here so he can sing for Scrooge!' William instructed the gang as the Christmasaurus began **bounding** down the Christmas-tree-lined path, pulling William up into the air.

'Hurry, there's not much time!' Santa's voice disappeared into the distance as the two friends shot towards the sky.

The grey clouds were as dark and thick as burnt porridge. It was a Scrooge-storm just waiting to burst! William could tell the Christmasaurus was too scared to fly anywhere near the clouds, just in case they were full of eerie Ebenezer-energy, so instead he swooped down low over the rooftops of Holly Heath, heading for the address Santa had given them.

The church clock seemed to be **tick-tocking** extra fast as they flew past. Time was running out!

Now, I know what you're thinking. Christmas Eve was already happening around the world and Santa hadn't delivered a single present yet! But, don't worry – if there's one thing that William and the Christmasaurus were experts at, it was saving Christmas, and all they needed to do was Christmas carol Scrooge, send him back to his book, restore the Christmas spirit that he had humbugged away, and then Santa and the Christmasaurus could speed back to the North Pole and start their deliveries!

Easy peasy!

'Do you know where Cobble Avenue is?' William called out over the cold wind *swooshing* by.

The Christmasaurus responded with a horse-like huff of air through his nostrils. He'd pulled Santa's sleigh with the reindeer enough times now to know his avenues from his cul-de-sacs (that's one of those funny roads

that don't lead anywhere!), so he knew exactly where Eddie Shepherd lived.

The Christmasaurus expertly weaved in and out of chimneys, then landed with a soft thud on the frosty stones of Cobble Avenue, right in front of a red-bricked house – just like Santa had described.

'**Whoa!**' William called, pulling on the tinsel until they came to a stop. 'This must be it, Chrissy – number twenty-six!'

They both looked at the house, which had dark windows, no wreath and no lights, then the Christmasaurus released a little nervous roar.

'You're right – it doesn't look very jingly! But Eddie Shepherd is the **jingliest Holly Jolly Jingler** of all. When he finds out Christmas is in danger, I know he'll help us,' William said as he rang the doorbell. 'It's probably best if you stay out of sight for a moment, Chrissy,' William added, suddenly remembering that not everyone was used to seeing a dinosaur on their doorstep on Christmas Eve.

The Christmasaurus looked around for a hiding place and let out a panicked squeak.

'I don't know! Hide anywhere! Behind a bush!' William hissed as a light flicked on inside. Someone was coming!

The Christmasaurus hopped into a flower bed and hid behind the first bush he found, just as the door opened, revealing Mr Shepherd, Eddie's dad.

''Ello, who's that? Sorry, I don't have my glasses on,' Mr Shepherd said, squinting at William.

'Hi, Mr Shepherd. My name's William. I go to school with Eddie – is he home?' William asked.

'He's just doing his homework. Can you come back another time?' Mr Shepherd asked as though it were any ordinary afternoon.

'**DOING HOMEWORK?**' William blurted out. 'But, Mr Shepherd, it's **Christmas Eve!**'

'Oh, is it? I hadn't noticed. Well, I suppose it's just as good as any other day for doing homework.' Mr Shepherd shrugged and started closing the door.

'No, wait! Please, I need to speak to Eddie – it's an emergency!' William pleaded.

'All right, but make it quick. After he's finished his homework, we're going to clean the house.' Then

Mr Shepherd disappeared inside and called for Eddie.

William's heart was racing now. Eddie was the missing piece to their Scrooge trap and, looking at the growing misery in the grey clouds above, Scrooge's power was only getting stronger. Christmas was in real danger!

'Hi, William,' said Eddie, sighing as he appeared at the door.

'Eddie!' William said. '**Thank goodness!** I've got good news and bad news.'

Eddie shrugged unenthusiastically. 'I suppose I'll have the good news first.'

William beamed at him. 'The Holly Jolly Jinglers Carol Concert *hasn't* been cancelled after all. It's back on – and so is your solo!'

'So, what's the good news?' Eddie asked.

William looked confused. 'That **IS** the good news. We still get to sing carols . . . on Christmas Eve!'

'Christmas? You don't still care about all that *stuff*, do you?' Eddie scoffed. 'Christmas is just a waste of time. Every idiot who goes about with "Merry Christmas" on his lips should be boiled with his own pudding!'

248

William froze: *boiled with his own pudding*? He knew those words; he'd heard them every time his dad had read him *A Christmas Carol*. And if Eddie was talking like Scrooge, that could only mean one thing . . .

'**You've been humbugged!**' William gasped.

Eddie frowned. 'I've been what?'

'There's no time to explain. Just stand there and listen.' Then William sat up straight, cleared his throat and started to sing.

'Once upon a Christmas,
In a little town,
No fairy lights were glowing
And people wore a frown.

But then it started snowing
And a child began to sing . . .'

Eddie's eyes started widening, as if he were waking up from a trance.

'W-W-William . . .' Eddie muttered.

'Yes? How do you feel? Has it worked?' William asked.

'There's a **D-D-DINOSAUR IN THE BUSH**!' Eddie screamed, leaping behind the door.

William turned to see that the bush the Christmasaurus had chosen to hide behind barely covered his bottom and he was standing there as clear as day!

'It's all right! Don't worry, Eddie. He's not going to eat you,' William said, trying not to laugh.

'You **KNOW** it?' Eddie squeaked, coming back into view.

'It's not an *it*. In fact, this is the one and only Christmasaurus!' William beamed and introduced his dino friend.

The Christmasaurus bounded over to William, standing tall and puffing out all his icicles.

'Awesome!' Eddie gasped. 'Can I stroke it? I mean,

can I stroke the Christmasaurus?'

'Why don't you ask him yourself?' William said.

'He can understand me?!' Eddie squeaked again, even louder.

William nodded.

'Can I stroke you?' Eddie nervously asked the Christmasaurus in awe.

His face lit up as the dinosaur bent his head low and leant in. And, as Eddie ran his fingers over the blue glassy shards of the Christmasaurus's mane, William couldn't help but notice a warm jingliness return to Eddie.

'This is the best Christmas ever!' Eddie whispered, and William knew then that all traces of Scrooginess had been de-humbugged.

Suddenly the church bell in the distance **DONGED** three clear **DONGS**. It was three o'clock!

'Wait, did you say the carol concert *isn't* cancelled?' Eddie asked.

'Yes! We need to get back to the bandstand! Christmas depends on it!' William said.

Eddie looked confused, clearly thinking, *How could Christmas depend on a carol concert?*

'Look around you,' William said. 'Christmas has been cancelled – maybe forever – but music might be the way to bring it back! I can explain everything, but remember when you said Christmas carols were like magic?'

Eddie nodded, recalling his words in the rehearsal room.

'Right now we *need* that magic. We need *you*. So let's go!'

And, at those words, the Christmasaurus bent down in front of Eddie.

'What's he doing?' said Eddie, looking at the dinosaur lying down in front of him.

William grinned. 'He wants to give you a ride.'

'Whoa, I've never ridden a dinosaur before. It's a bit icy, though. He won't slip on the roads, will he?' Eddie asked as he climbed on to the Christmasaurus's back.

'Roads? Where we're going, we don't need –'

But before William could finish what he was saying, the Christmasaurus had **scooped** up the tinsel-reins and burst into a gallop, flying up into the sky with Eddie on his back and William soaring behind them as they raced to save Christmas.

CHAPTER TWENTY-SEVEN
SCROOGE

The Christmasaurus landed on the bandstand with Eddie and William.

'You made it!' Santa said, beaming. 'Of course, I always knew you would! And you must be Eddie! I've heard all about your singing. Pleased to meet you. I'm –'

'**Santa!**' Eddie said, blinking in disbelief.

William had mentioned Santa to Eddie on the way to the square. But, even so, coming face to face with the actual legendary Santa was still a lot to take in!

Santa chuckled. **'Ho-ho-ho! Indeed I am!'**

'Where are the other Holly Jolly Jinglers?' Eddie asked, looking around for the rest of the choir. 'Where're Marcus, Grace and Kai?'

'They're not coming,' William confessed.

'You mean, it's just you and me?' Eddie asked.

'Actually, it's just *you*. It's a long story.' William was about to explain about the big solo that Eddie was going to sing when –

BANG!

A loud noise crashed through the trees, making everyone jump.

The whole gang instantly huddled together, looking in all directions, trying to see whatever or whoever had made that sound.

CRASH!

There was another one, followed by a rustle in the trees.

'Can anyone see anything?' William shouted.

'Nothing over this side!' replied Lucy, pulling on her adventure goggles again.

'Nothing here either!' confirmed Brenda.

An eerie stillness suddenly fell around them, as if the air had been frozen.

'William, this isn't what the Christmas carol concert is normally like,' Eddie whispered.

'This isn't going to be a normal Christmas carol concert,' William replied.

Suddenly one of the Christmas lights at the end of a row of trees exploded like a tiny blue firework in the distance.

'It's OK – there are plenty of lights. It doesn't matter if we lose a few,' Bob reassured everyone.

The next light in the chain blew in a flash of red.

The lights started exploding, one by one, along the wires they'd hung round the town square.

Blue sparks, red sparks, gold sparks, all bursting along from lamp post to lamp post, getting faster and faster as the explosions wound their way closer to where everyone was huddled –

POP! POP! POP!

– not stopping until every tiny little bulb of beautiful brilliance had been burst.

With one final **POP!** sparks fell to the ground like glowing snow. Sparks that were a familiar shade of green that William recognized in an instant. They were the exact same colour as the cover of the book that was still stowed away under his chair. It could only mean one thing: Scrooge was drawing closer!

'Will someone explain what's going on?' Eddie cried, and everyone looked to William.

'All right.' William took a deep breath, about to do another one of his super-fast explanations. 'Ebenezer Scrooge has escaped from a magical copy of *A Christmas Carol* and he's now on the loose, trying to *humbug* everything Christmassy and rewrite a new ending to his story where he can keep living his miserable, wicked life in a world with **NO CHRISTMAS**, and we're the only ones who can stop him!'

Eddie replied with a very slow blink as he tried to take in what William had just told him.

But there wasn't time for any more details, as a chilly breeze began to snake through the trees, bouncing the baubles from the branches and twangling all the tinsel into knots.

'He must be near!' Santa mumbled through a mouthful of his own bushy beard that had blown into his face.

Then, as the breeze became a gust, William caught glimpses of something in the shadows through the shivering tree bristles . . . but the next moment it was gone.

'I think we'd better get into *jingling* positions!' Bob said.

The gang quickly huddled into the centre of the stage, ready for the last stand against Scrooge.

'Eddie, you're front and centre. Me, Brenda and Lucy will be right behind you,' William said, as Brenda and Lucy gave Eddie a nervous but supportive thumbs up.

'We're right behind you too!' Bob said, introducing himself to Eddie with the Jingler's Salute (which William was pretty sure his dad had just made up).

'Ex-Jingler Bob Trundle, ready for carol service.'

Pamela and Larry lined up beside Bob, while Santa and the Christmasaurus stood together in the middle, shielded by the others. They couldn't be too careful – after all, the world needed Santa!

'OK, everyone – this is it,' announced William. 'We are all that stands between Scrooge and Santa, and we must protect Christmas at all costs. No matter what you do, keep thinking Christmassy thoughts, keep the spirit of Christmas alive and, most important of all, **_KEEP SINGING_**!'

Suddenly the Christmasaurus started sniffing the air as if he'd caught a whiff of something evil, and he began to growl at the trees.

'If only we could see what's on the other side of those trees,' Lucy said. Then William had an idea.

'Chrissy, why don't you fly up and tell us what you see?' William suggested. 'You can get a bird's-eye view.'

'You mean a dino's-eye view,' Santa said, chuckling.

'Exactly! And let us know when Scrooge is coming,' said William.

The Christmasaurus quickly whooshed into the air

above the square, peering down into the Christmas trees, looking for signs of Scrooge.

'Can you see anything, Christmasaurus?' William called up, but the Christmasaurus just shook his head – nothing.

He flew in circles high above the bandstand, looking around and around, getting further and further away from the huddled gang until he disappeared up into the grey clouds overhead. Soon, William couldn't see his blue friend in the sky any more.

'Christmasaurus?' William called.

There was no reply.

'Can anyone see him at all? Where's he gone? Christmasaurus!' William shouted.

This time there was a reply – only it wasn't the one William wanted. It came as a faint whisper on the cold breeze. Just one word: **'HUMBUG!'**

The gang pulled in closer. There was no doubt any more that Scrooge had arrived, and now William's best friend was out there somewhere.

'I see something!' Lucy yelled, pointing into the thick layer of Christmas trees.

'I see it too,' said Brenda. 'It's the Christmasaurus!'

William breathed a sigh of relief. His friend hadn't vanished after all. But as the dinosaur stepped through the row of pines, William's heart froze. Something was wrong. Very wrong.

The Christmasaurus had changed and every scale from his snout to the tip of his tail was glowing green.

'No!' William cried, but it was too late.

The Christmasaurus had been **humbugged**! His eyes were glossed over as though he were under some sort of Scroogey spell.

But that wasn't the worst part.

As this new anti-Christmasaurus stepped further out of the trees, William saw that there was someone riding on his friend's back. Someone crooked and cold, someone wicked and old, someone who didn't belong in this world.

Ebenezer Scrooge.

Chapter Twenty-Eight
SANTA'S LAST WORDS

There was a ghostly silence as the Christmas gang stared at this transformed ghastly green Christmasaurus and the man riding on his scaly back.

Scrooge's clothes were as black as soot, and his skin as grey as the swirling clouds above them. His eyes were hidden in the shadow cast by the brim of his top hat, only made visible because they seemed to be radiating the same green glow as the Christmasaurus's glassy scales.

'Get off my friend!' William called out, the words flying out of his mouth before he could stop them.

Scrooge said nothing, but the Christmasaurus huffed a puff of cold air through his nostrils in response and a wicked smile crept across Scrooge's thin lips.

In fact, it was hard to call it a smile. It was more like an unwanted crack appearing in a frozen lake, slicing at an angle across his hard, icy features.

Reading about Scrooge in a story was frightening enough, but seeing the actual man with his very eyes was just about the scariest thing William had ever experienced. It's **almost too horrible** for me to write in this story, but in case you're wondering what it might feel like to come face to face with Scrooge riding a dinosaur, try to imagine being so absolutely terrified that you can't move. Not even a twitch of the tiniest muscle. Even if you really, really needed to go to the toilet, you'd be too scared to move from the spot you were on, as if you were stuck to it and might have to stay there for the rest of your petrified existence.

That's how **spine-tinglingly scary** Scrooge was, but that didn't stop William, not when the Christmasaurus was in trouble! It was time to put their plan into action!

'This is it. Eddie, you need to start singing,' William said, trying to keep his voice steady.

Eddie gulped.

'You can do it!' urged William. 'You've got the best voice in the whole school.'

Brenda turned to Eddie and said encouragingly, 'I've never heard you sing but I believe in you!'

'Me too!' added Lucy.

'B-b-but I'm ... nervous!'

Eddie replied, trembling. 'For the first time ever I think I've got stage fright!'

'I know exactly how you're feeling right now,' said William, putting a reassuring hand on the Holly Jolly Jingler's arm.

'Y-you do?' said Eddie.

'Yeah! That's how nervous I felt after the first time I heard **YOU** sing. I wanted the solo more than anything in the world, but after hearing how awesome you were, I just wanted to be invisible,' William explained.

'I'd love to be invisible right now,' whispered Eddie, still trembling.

'Well, luckily for us, that's impossible! It's now or never – let's jingle Scrooge back to where he belongs!' said William, pulling out the magical copy of *A Christmas Carol* from his chair.

SANTA'S LAST WORDS

At the sight of the book, the Christmasaurus released a mighty roar, and the icy crack of a smile that had appeared on Scrooge's face instantly froze over.

'I don't think he likes that book,' Bob whispered.

'He will . . . He just needs to get to the end. It's a Christmas story – everything is *always* all right in the end,' said William, and with that he gave Eddie an encouraging nod.

It was time.

Eddie took a breath and started to sing the Holly Jolly Jinglers' carol.

'Once upon a Christmas,
In a little town,
No fairy lights were glowing
And people wore a frown.

But then it started snowing
And a child began to sing,
Spreading Christmas joy
To everyone and everything . . .'

269

As Eddie's voice rose in the town square, Scrooge began frowning and covering his ears as though he were trying to escape the carol.

'Ho-ho! I think it's starting to work!'

boomed Santa, popping his head over his friends to take a look.

Scrooge's beady green eyes spotted Santa in a flash, like a snake targeting its prey. The sight of the most Christmassy person in the universe seemed to ignite a spark of wretchedness within Scrooge, sending him to a whole new level of Scrooginess.

'HUMBUG!'

he screeched, his high-pitched voice scraping through the air like nails across a chalkboard, creating a shockwave of misery that blasted across the square.

The needles on all the Christmas trees instantly turned brown and fell to the ground, leaving the gang in a forest of bare branches, surrounded by the skeletons of the pines.

'Keep singing, Eddie!' William shouted. 'Eddie . . . ?'

William tapped his friend on the shoulder. Eddie turned to him, and William saw that his eyes were glowing the same green as Scrooge's!

Eddie had been humbugged!

'No!' William gasped. 'Quick, we all need to sing together to bring him back!'

But there was no reply.

'Brenda? Lucy?' William called, but it was too late. They staggered from the bandstand – they'd been humbugged too!

And so had everyone else! Bob, Pamela, Larry – the whole gang were under Scrooge's hypnotic spell, with green eyes set in faces as solemn as the first Monday of January.

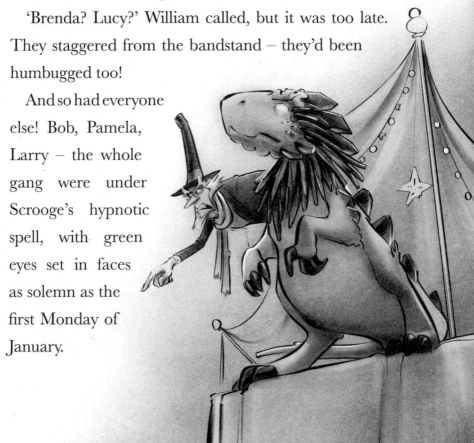

'I . . . I . . . feel all funny,' Santa croaked, and William watched as his rosy cheeks faded to grey and his red suit turned green.

'Santa, not you too!' cried William. 'What about Christmas?'

Santa looked William in the eyes and said two words that broke his heart:

'Who cares.'

Chapter Twenty-Nine
HUMBUG

The town square was no longer the magical winter wonderland that it had been just a few moments before. Now, it looked more like a battlefield after an epic winter war between Christmas and Scrooge – and it appeared as though Christmas was losing!

Scrooge climbed down from the Christmasaurus's back like some sort of dark knight dismounting his horse after a long journey from a faraway realm of misery. He ran his greedy fingers over the dinosaur's green scales as though they were valuable gems that he could now hoard along with the rest of his precious wealth.

All the while, the Christmasaurus stared ahead with wide green eyes. Scrooge sneered at the bare trees, then he turned his attention to William. Slowly, the crooked miser took a step towards the bandstand where the last remaining decorations hung, but he stopped when he spotted what William was holding: *the book*.

'You're afraid of this, aren't you?' William called out, holding on tight to the mysterious novel.

'Bah, humbug!'

Scrooge scoffed, as though the very idea of being afraid was total nonsense, but William could tell by the way the man never took his eyes off the golden letters on the worn cover that Scrooge didn't want to come any closer to the story he'd escaped from.

William knew he had to find a way to get Scrooge back inside the pages in his hands, but with everyone else now humbugged, there was no one to help. William was on his own. Solo.

SOLO . . . William thought to himself.

Eddie couldn't sing – that was clear – but Bob's confession about his own solo with the Holly Jolly Jinglers flashed through William's mind. Bob might not have been chosen to sing, but when his friend forgot the words, he stepped in and saved the day.

William looked at Eddie and realized that this was his chance to follow in his dad's footsteps and have that Christmas solo after all!

William braced himself, rolled up to the bandstand, then opened the book. Scrooge hissed and cowered.

'You don't need to be afraid,' William said to him. 'It's just a story – *your* story. Even though it's scary to see what's on the next page, you just have to trust that everything will be all right in the end.'

Scrooge's face creased into a scowl, and William took a deep breath and began to sing:

'Once upon a Christmas,
In a little town,
No fairy lights were glowing
And people wore a frown . . .'

William's voice rang out, filling the square. Curiously, the melody seemed to stir up some sort of magic in the book. Its pages started fluttering, as if there were a storm contained within, trying to reach out.

Scrooge panicked and unleashed his mightiest *humbug* yet.

'HUMBUUUUUUUUG!'

he cried to the clouds above.

Bright lightning flashed through the sky, followed by a giant rumble of thunder, which caused the ground to shake so hard that the book slipped from William's hands and abruptly slammed shut as it hit the stage. Whatever magic William's Christmas carol had conjured up was immediately stopped.

William reached down to grab the book, but Scrooge was quicker. A crooked smile cracked across his icy features and another bolt of lightning fuelled by Ebenezer-energy struck the bandstand, **zapping** William with a stroke of pure misery as he squeezed his eyes shut against the blinding flash.

Thunder rumbled once more and William opened his eyes.

A green glow radiated from them, and everything

looked a little different . . . A little darker. A little colder. A little *Scroogier.*

William Trundle had been humbugged!

As he looked around at the town square with his new Scrooge-Vision, William had never felt so wretched in all his life. Everything was gloriously glum now that Scrooge's miserable magic had destroyed most of the decorations.

'Humbug!' William spat, the word flying out of his mouth as he plucked a bauble that hung from the side of the bandstand and placed it on the stage before rolling over it with his wheelchair.

CRUNCH!

The crumbling decoration sent a shiver of Scrooginess through him and it felt good . . . I mean, *bad* . . . I mean, so bad that it was good!

As if inspired by his Scrooginess, everyone else started ripping down the remaining decorations. Brenda, Eddie, Lucy, Larry, Pamela and Bob – the whole gang suddenly sought to destroy every last piece of Christmas sparkle.

Even Santa took a candy cane down and snapped it in two.

'**Pah-ha-ha!**' Scrooge cackled. 'Your pathetic little song didn't work, and now you and your friends have forgotten the meaning of this idiotic time of year. We can finally live in a world where there is no Christmas! Humbug!'

'Humbug!' cheered William like some sort of zombie.

'*Humbug!*' everyone else moaned in unison.

Well, everyone except for . . . the Christmasaurus.

Scrooge paused, his ears pricking up like a hound at the silence from behind.

'*HUMBUG!*'

Scrooge repeated, turning to scowl at the Christmasaurus.

And, when he did, Scrooge saw that the green humbugged Christmasaurus was gone. Instead, there was something brilliant and blue standing triumphantly in the clearing.

The Christmasaurus was back.

CHAPTER THIRTY

A CHRISTMASAURUS CAROL

'I – I . . . don't understand . . .' Scrooge spluttered, staring at the restored Christmasaurus, who was back to his shimmery blue self, glistening brightly amid the forest of skeleton Christmas trees. 'The boy's carol wasn't powerful enough to defeat me! How is this possible?'

Scrooge was right: William's solo *hadn't* been powerful enough to send him back into the pages of his story, but the Christmas carol had floated into the Christmasaurus's ears, where its warm, festive magic had flowed through the dino's scales, melting away all traces of humbug.

The Christmasaurus shook his icicles like a wet dog and stood looking more Christmassy than ever as he fixed his deep blue eyes on Scrooge and started to growl.

The Christmasaurus might have been the first dinosaur Scrooge had ever met, but the man didn't need a translator to understand what this growl meant: *GET AWAY FROM MY FRIENDS!*

Scrooge's eyes narrowed, getting ready to target his next humbug, but before he could even utter *HUM*, the Christmasaurus blasted a mighty *ROAR!* that knocked the top hat right off Ebenezer's grumpy old head.

While Scrooge dusted the snow from his hat, the Christmasaurus turned his attention to William and the rest of the gang, who were still busy destroying the decorations on the bandstand.

His tail fell with sadness. He needed to do something. Something that would make them remember the wonder of Christmas. Something magical . . . Something miraculous . . . Something . . . *MUSICAL!*

The scales on the Christmasaurus's neck perked up

as he realized that what he had to do was SING!

He didn't know how to; he'd never done it before, and he wasn't even sure if dinosaurs *could* sing, but he had to give it a try. Christmas and his friends were depending on him!

So the Christmasaurus took a deep breath of Christmas Eve air, lifted his head to the sky and began to roar a song.

And this was no ordinary Christmas carol. This was a **Christmasaurus Carol**! His roar was somewhere between a wolf's howl and a whale call, beautifully haunting and full of wonder. As the melody reached the sky, it seemed to evaporate the storm clouds, revealing an incredible Christmas Eve sky full of the late afternoon's first stars, which shone their light over the square.

Scrooge covered his ears, unable to bear the intense Christmassy tune as it washed over the bandstand, reawakening the humbugged gang, one by one.

William was the first to snap out of Scrooge's miserable magic, shaking his head as if he'd been having a bad dream.

'Christmasaurus?' William said, rubbing the final glow of green away from his eyes, hardly able to believe what he was seeing as his dinosaur friend continued to howl his tune at the sky.

'What's he doing?' asked Brenda.

'My goodness, I do believe he's **SINGING**!' gasped Santa.

Suddenly the fallen pine needles from the destroyed Christmas trees began to rise off the ground, floating into the air around the Christmasaurus and re-attaching themselves to the skeletal branches. The Christmasaurus's carol was *reversing* Scrooge's miserable magic and bringing Christmas back to life!

'Nooo!' howled Scrooge, looking around in dismay.

'Humbug! Humbug!'

A Christmasaurus Carol

But no one was listening any more. The power of the music was too strong.

'The trees are alive again!' Bob cheered.

'Then let's start decorating them!' Lucy cried.

'But how?' said Larry. 'I think we smashed all the decorations!' He looked sadly at the shards of broken baubles at his feet.

'There's only one way to reverse this mess,' William said with a smile.

'Carolling!' exclaimed Eddie.

The two boys grinned at each other and joined in with the Christmasaurus.

> 'Lighting up the night,
> Candles shining bright,
> A Christmas carol
> Will fill the world with light.
>
> At this time of year,
> Any time you hear
> A Christmas carol,
> You will feel the Christmas cheer!'

All of a sudden the copy of *A Christmas Carol*, which was resting on the frosty stage, flew open and a strong wind gusted through the square.

HUMBUG!

HUMBUG!

HUMBUG!'

Scrooge shrieked as the wind took the hat from his head. All eyes were on it as it swirled in the air and then down towards the book, where it vanished into the open pages.

'It's too late for that now, Scrooge!' Santa called.

'Yeah! We're the Christmas pest control and we specialize in exterminating *humBUGS*!' Brenda said in her toughest voice.

'You've been waiting to say that, haven't you?' William whispered to her.

'All night!' replied Brenda with a wink.

In the next instant, the swirling, whirling Christmas storm blew so hard that the book itself was picked up in the gale.

'The book!' shouted Eddie.

'Somebody grab it!' Pamela screamed as everyone scrambled and tumbled over each other, reaching and clawing in the air for the escaping novel.

William wheeled himself towards it as fast as he could, the blustering breeze giving him an extra boost of speed, but, just as the green spine of the book was at his fingertips, his wheelchair hit a stone and tipped forward. He tumbled out of his chair and through the air, but he had only one thing on his mind:

CATCH THAT BOOK!

His eyes set on the book, William reached out and snatched it from the air, before squeezing his eyes shut, ready to hit the ground . . .

Only the ground never came.

Instead, when he opened his eyes, he discovered that he was sitting on the scaly blue back of the Christmasaurus.

'You caught me!' William cheered as they flew around the bandstand, and the Christmasaurus let out a mighty roar.

'Now, let's carol Scrooge back to his own story!' William cried to the others on the bandstand.

The Christmasaurus swooped back to the ground, and William held the book open again as the rest of the Christmas gang started to sing.

The Christmas carol rang out in the square. Within seconds, the wind picked up even more and Scrooge was pulled towards William and the open book.

'It's working!'

yelled Brenda.

'Keep singing!' William said, and everyone belted out the carol at the top of their voices.

A Christmasaurus Carol

'Lighting up the night,
Candles shining bright,
A Christmas carol
Will fill the world with light . . .'

It didn't matter if they were singing in tune, or if they sang the wrong words; it didn't matter if they sounded good or bad – that's not the point of Christmas carols. Just like Eddie had said, it's impossible for anyone to hear a carol and not feel Christmassy, and now the Holly Jolly Jinglers' song was bringing them all together with pure joy and filling the air with Christmas cheer.

The wind whipped on, and Scrooge lost his footing at last, sliding towards the open book in William's hands, grasping, scraping, clutching at anything he could as he tried to stay in this world.

The Christmasaurus dug his claws into the ground, holding William steady on his back so he could keep the book open as mysterious swirling green magic drew Scrooge closer and closer.

'It's time for you to finish your own story now, Scrooge. To learn the true meaning of Christmas,'

William shouted over the swirling winds. 'Your future is within *these* pages!'

As the carollers reached the final chorus of their song, Scrooge suddenly stared at the group of friends in a way that William hadn't seen before.

He studied their warm, kind faces carefully, observing Bob and Pamela holding hands, and Larry placing a loving arm round his daughter, while Eddie and Brenda linked arms and swayed to the carol as they sang. Scrooge saw friends and family

singing together in the face of pure misery and, as the howling winds grew too intense for the man to bear, he looked William deep in the eye and spoke:

'I know your purpose is to do me good, and I hope to live to be another man from what I was.'

And, with those words, Scrooge surrendered to the gravity of his story and was pulled into the pages. Without hesitation, William slammed the book shut.

Ebenezer Scrooge was **gone**.

CHAPTER THIRTY-ONE

THE CHRISTMAS THAT ALMOST NEVER WAS

There was stillness in the air as everyone stared at the closed book in William's hands.

'We did it!' he cheered.

Bob picked up the overturned wheelchair and moved it towards the Christmasaurus. William slid down the dinosaur's scaly tail, landing safely back in his chair.

Everyone huddled round, taking turns to examine the book while they celebrated with hugs and high fives.

'Is it really over? Has Scrooge gone?' Eddie asked, carefully flicking through the pages as though Scrooge might fall out.

'I believe so!' Santa said, smiling. 'He's returned to fulfil his destiny and live out the end of his story the way it was always meant to happen.'

'Well, it was all thanks to some amazing carolling!' Bob said, beaming at William.

'I wish I could take the credit, but it was the Christmasaurus's singing that really saved the day,' William said, and if it were possible for dinosaurs to blush, then the blue dinosaur would have turned as red as Santa's suit.

'Yes, the power of music, especially Christmas music, is a marvellous thing,' Santa said, and as he spoke there was a faint sound in the distance.

'What's that noise?' Pamela asked.

'It's . . . *singing!*'

Bob cried.

'My goodness, you're right! Look, carollers!' Santa beamed with joy as the people of Holly Heath (and a few from the edge of Whiffington too!) began gathering in the town square, singing the Holly Jolly Jinglers' carol.

296

'Lighting up the night,
Candles shining bright,
A Christmas carol
Will fill the world with light.

At this time of year,
Any time you hear
A Christmas carol,
You will feel the Christmas cheer!'

Familiar faces could be seen among the crowd of carollers: Marcus, Grace and Kai and all the Holly Jolly Jinglers. Even Miss Melody was there, conducting the townsfolk with merry tears in her eyes.

Within minutes, the town square was full of happy people singing together, and as William looked around, he realized something.

'All the decorations are back!' he said, and he was right.

Every single cane, bauble, tinsel string and star that had lain destroyed on the ground a moment ago now sparkled out from the branches of the restored trees and the outside of the bandstand. The Christmas lights that had exploded were now glistening as good as new and, as everyone glanced up, they saw there wasn't a cloud in the sky – only stars twinkling overhead.

'Look at the houses too!' Brenda shouted, pointing to the homes that surrounded the town square. Each one was now lit with flashing lights, and fully decorated trees could be seen through the windows.

'I suppose you'd better start delivering some presents soon, Santa . . . Santa?' said Bob. But when he turned round, he discovered that there was nothing but footprints in the snow where Santa and the Christmasaurus had been standing.

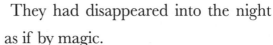

They had disappeared into the night as if by magic.

'**They've gone!**' Lucy gasped.

The Christmas gang started looking for any sign of Santa and the Christmasaurus. Everyone except William, that is. He knew to look up to the clear sky, where he spotted a single shooting star with a blue trail zooming across the night, heading north, as the townsfolk joyously sang the final verse of the Jinglers' carol as loud as they could.

'Oh, don't worry – it's Christmas Eve, remember? They'll be back on your roof in a few hours,' William said, grinning.

'As long as you're on the **Nice List**!' Brenda added.

'After tonight I think you're *all* on the Nice List forever!' Bob smiled, and the kids cheered in agreement.

From across the square, Miss Melody spotted Bob and instantly came bounding over.

'If it isn't my favourite Holly Jolly Jingler, Bob Trundle!' she cooed. 'Oh, and what's that book you have there, William?' she asked, spotting the unusual green cover in William's hands.

'It's *A Christmas Carol*,' William said, showing it to her.

'Oh, how **perfect**!' Miss Melody's face lit up. 'Ah, I have an idea! This is the very story for Christmas Eve. Gather round, everyone!' she called out. 'It's time for a reading! Bob, would you do the honours?'

Before he could respond, Miss Melody ushered Bob up to the bandstand and shoved the book into his hands as the crowd gathered round, ready for a Christmas story.

'Dad, are you sure it's safe?' William whispered.

'I think Scrooge is ready to hear his ending, don't you?' Bob said quietly with a smile.

With the whole town listening, with cups of hot chocolate and mulled wine, Bob began reading the story that had started it all. He transformed himself into all the characters as only Bob Trundle could, acting out Scrooge and all three spirits as he read under the stars, showing everyone how that miserable miser Scrooge became the most **Christmas-loving** man in all of London.

When he reached the end, Bob closed the book to rapturous applause.

'Oh, Bob! What a wonderful reading! The perfect Christmas Eve story,' Miss Melody cheered.

THE CHRISTMAS THAT ALMOST NEVER WAS

Eddie let out a long, exhausted yawn. 'I think I'd better go home, or I won't be asleep when Santa comes!'

'Us too,' said Larry. 'We should be heading back to Whiffington!'

'Thanks for a **brilliant adventure**!' Lucy said as she hugged William, Brenda and Eddie goodbye.

And, with one last look, they all left the party in the town square as the townsfolk merrily celebrated the Christmas that almost never was.

'**G**oodnight, Eddie!' William waved as they reached his friend's house, which was now covered with decorations.

'Night, William. Goodnight, Brenda. Oh, and William – you've got a great voice. I think you might even have a shot at getting the Jinglers' solo next Christmas,' Eddie said with a wink.

'Well, maybe next year it should be a duet?' William suggested, and a huge smile spread across Eddie's face.

'Deal!' he said before disappearing into his house.

As the Trundles made their way back through town, they passed all the redecorated homes of Holly Heath.

The Cawleys' garden was full of lit-up elves again, Mrs Jones's snowmen statues were once more dancing on the garage roof, and Mr Ridley's good old plastic singing Christmas tree was **fa-la-la-la-ing** in his driveway.

'All back to normal,' William said, smiling.

Then he suddenly spotted something out of the corner of his eye. Something out of place. A building that he could have sworn wasn't there a few seconds ago.

'It's the **Night-Before Library**!' he gasped. 'It's back!'

'Looks like it's closed, though,' said Brenda. 'I guess you'll have to hold on to that book a little longer, William.'

'Maybe not – there's a sign next to the door,' said Pamela, pointing to a golden plaque that read:

'So *that's* why it's called the *Night-Before Library!*' William exclaimed.

'Good job it's the night before Christmas . . .' said Pamela with a smile.

'And that we've got plenty of Christmas trees!' Bob added as the Trundles left the mysterious library and continued on their festive way home.

Just a short while later they were back inside their warm, wonky home and dressed in their best festive pyjamas. As Brenda and Pamela left a mince pie and a carrot next to the chimney and Bob hung up everyone's stockings (even one for Growler!), William carefully placed the old copy of *A Christmas Carol* under the tree.

Then they all wished each other a merry Christmas Eve before finally going to bed for one of the best sleeps ever.

For the first time in years, William did not wake up when Santa and the Christmasaurus landed on their roof. Instead, he slept soundly through the night and then stirred slowly in the morning, for a moment completely forgetting what day it was until . . .

'IT'S CHRIIIIISTMAAAAAAAAS!'

Bob's excited voice boomed merrily from the hallway. 'Wakey, wakey, rise and shine! Get out of bed, it's **CHRISTMAS TIME**!'

Bob, Pamela, Brenda, William and Growler all gathered in the living room where they found a small pile of perfectly wrapped presents under the tree for William and another for Brenda.

But before they could open their presents, William noticed something.

'The book – it's gone!' he said.

'Yes, and look, there's something else under the tree,' said Bob.

In the spot where the book had been, there was now a tall, black top hat that could only have belonged to one person: SCROOGE!

'What's *that* doing here?' William gasped.

'I don't know!' Bob whispered nervously.

'You don't think he could have come back, do you?' asked Pamela, glancing around the room.

'Wait – what's that sticking out of his hat?' said Brenda, pointing at a tiny piece of tea-coloured paper that was poking out of the trim.

William picked out the piece of paper and unfolded it to find a handwritten note on the other side, which he read aloud:

'I will honour Christmas in my heart, and try to keep it all the year. I will live in the Past, the Present and the Future. The Spirits of all Three shall strive within me.'

Ebenezer Scrooge

THE CHRISTMAS THAT ALMOST NEVER WAS

'Merry Christmas, Ebenezer Scrooge!' William said, smiling at the thought of the old man who had finally reached the happy ending of his story, just as you have reached the end of this one.

THE END

ACKNOWLEDGEMENTS

Hello, all – it's Tom here. Yes, the one whose name is on the front of this book, in big shiny letters, because I wrote all the words inside it. BUT the truth is there should be a whole list of names on the front, as this book would not exist without the amazing team that I am very lucky to be part of. With that in mind, I would like to thank . . .

Shane Devries for using his magical talent to bring this story to life. These are the most beautiful books I've ever seen, and it's all because of Shane.

Special thanks to Natalie Doherty, who has left the team for new adventures. Nat has been a fundamental part of The Christmasaurus from day one. Thanks for believing that Chrissy could fly!

My brilliant manager, Rachel Drake, for dealing with my dramas and properly looking after me and my world.

Stephanie Thwaites, my awesome agent, for always believing in my weird words. To Grace Robinson and the whole team at Curtis Brown.

And now to the talented people at Puffin:

Firstly to Jane Griffiths for leaping down the chimney and into this book while I was halfway through writing it!

The editorial elves: India Chambers, Shreeta Shah, Wendy Shakespeare, Debbie Hatfield, Toria Hegedus and George Maudsley.

The design elves: Emily Smyth and the team at Dynamo.

The production pixies: Adam Webling and Naomi Green.

The sales elves: Geraldine McBride, Kat Baker, Toni Budden, Rozzie Todd and Becki Wells.

The rights elves: Alice Grigg and Maeve Banham.

The marketing/PR elves: Lottie Halsted and Harriet Venn.

The audio elf: Stella Newing.

Endless thanks to Tom Weldon, Francesca Dow and Amanda Punter for believing in me as an author and letting me be part of the PRH family.

To Michael Gracey for the constant Christmas inspiration and for always challenging me to be better. To Fletch for spreading the Christmasaurus magic from day one.

Thanks to all the McFLY guys, Matt Milton and the whole McFLY family. Thanks to all GDs who have supported me from music to books.

To Lou, Susana and Jorge for looking after my life and my family.

My parents and sister for giving me magical, inspiring childhood Christmases.

Thanks to my wonderful wife, Giovanna, for all the love and patience, and to my three boys, Buzz, Buddy and Max for listening to my ideas first. Special thanks to Buzz for reading this story before anyone else and spotting all my mistakes!

Finally, you, the reader. I can't thank you enough for coming on this adventure, and I hope your time spent in the world within my words has been enjoyable.

Merry Christmas!

Tom

Ready for some
Christmasaurus festive fun?

Keep reading . . .

DINO-RRIFIC
DECORATIONS

Here's the Christmasaurus's favourite fun way to make fantastic decorations for the Christmas tree. Once, the Christmasaurus actually tried to eat these and his dino-tummy was very unhappy afterwards. These decorations are definitely just for looking at and not for chomping on! Just like Snowcrumb's recipes, it's best to ask a grown-up for permission and help, especially when using a hot oven.

What you need:

Makes 10–12 decorations

- A baking tray
- Greaseproof paper
- 250 g plain flour, with a little extra for dusting
- 125 g table salt (fine salt is best)
- A bowl
- 125 g water
- A wooden spoon
- A rolling pin
- Biscuit cutters (any shape will do, but the more Christmassy, the better!)
- A pencil or pen
- Felt-tip pens, paints or eco-friendly glitter for decoration
- String or thin ribbon

What to do:

1 With the permission and help of a grown-up, preheat the oven to its lowest setting and line a baking tray with greaseproof paper.

2 Mix the flour and salt in a bowl. Add the water gradually, and stir with a wooden spoon until the mixture comes together into a ball.

3 Lightly dust a clean surface with flour, and then move the dough ball to the floured surface. Using your rolling pin, roll the dough out flat until it's around a centimetre thick. (If you don't have a rolling pin, you can always use your hands to press the dough flat.)

4 Press biscuit cutters into the dough to cut out shapes.

5 With the tip of a pencil or pen, poke a small hole in the top of each shape.

6 Carefully place your shapes on to the baking tray.

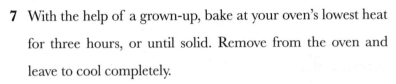

7 With the help of a grown-up, bake at your oven's lowest heat for three hours, or until solid. Remove from the oven and leave to cool completely.

8 Now for the fun part! Once your shapes have cooled, you can paint and decorate them any way you like. Paint that has a sprinkling of glitter looks dino-tastic!

9 When your decorations are completely dry, push a piece of string or ribbon through the hole at the top of each shape and tie in a knot. Now your homemade decorations are ready to hang on your Christmas tree!

MERRY MINCE PIES!

A Christmas classic.

Ingredients

Makes 24 perfect mince pies

260 g unsalted butter, softened

375 g plain flour, plus a sprinkle extra for dusting

125 g caster sugar, plus a little extra for dusting

2 large eggs

800 g jar of mincemeat

Snowcrumb's steps

1 Wash your hands really well with water and lots of soap.

2 Ask a grown-up to help you cut the softened butter into 2-centimetre squares, and then add it to a mixing bowl with the flour.

3 Use your fingers to rub the ingredients together until the mixture looks like breadcrumbs.

4 Add one egg and the sugar to the bowl, and then mix everything together thoroughly.

5 Lightly dust a clean surface with flour, and then tip the mixture out on to the floured surface.

6 Fold the mixture until the pastry comes together – try not to over-mix it. As soon as it easily forms a ball, you're done!

7 Wrap the pastry up in cling film and pop it into the fridge to rest for 15 minutes or so.

8   With the permission and help of a grown-up, preheat your oven to 220 degrees Celsius and grease a cupcake tray (you can use a little butter or a light spray of oil).

9   Lightly flour your surface again, and roll out the pastry to about 3 millimetres thick. While rolling it out, make sure to turn the pastry 90 degrees between rolling – it will help stop the mixture from sticking to the surface and will make sure you get an even thickness. If the pastry does begin to stick, add a little more flour to the surface.

10 Use a round cutter (about 10 centimetres) to cut out 24 bases and place them gently into your cupcake trays. To make sure the pastry gets right down into the tray, use a little bit of rolled-up pastry to gently push in each base.

11 Push a tablespoon or so of mincemeat into each base.

12 Re-roll your remaining pastry, and use a smaller round cutter (about 7 centimetres) to cut some lids.

13 Crack the second egg into a small dish, then brush the edges of your mince-pie bases with a little egg before placing on the lids. Press the edges of the lids down to seal them to the base.

14 With the help of a grown-up, bake the mince pies for 15–20 minutes – you will know they are ready when they are golden brown and bubbling. **YUM.**

15 Cool the mince pies on a wire rack for a minute or two before removing them from the tray. Once they've cooled slightly, remove them from the tray and place on a wire rack to cool completely.

16 Using a sift, dust the top of the mince pies with a little bit of caster sugar. Enjoy!

Check out

THE CHRISTMASAURUS CRACKER

for more activities
and puzzles!

Have you read all of Tom Fletcher's Brilliant Stories?

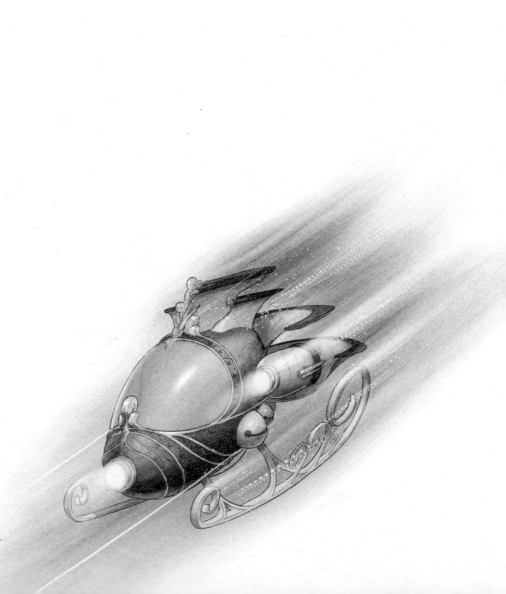